MATTER OUT OF PLACE

Western Literature and Fiction Series

Like the iconic physical landscape and diverse cultures that inspire it, the literature of the American West is imbued with power and beauty. The Western Literature and Fiction Series invites scholarship reflecting on the authors and works that define the creative expression of the past and present while championing the literary fiction that propels us forward.

The Desert Between Us
Phyllis Barber

The Brightest Place in the World
David Philip Mullins

This Here Is Devil's Work
Curtis Bradley Vickers

The Ghost Dancers
Adrian C. Louis

Skins
Adrian C. Louis

Drowning in the Desert
Bernard Schopen

No Charity in the Wilderness: Poems
Shaun T. Griffin

Dream City: A Novel
Douglas Unger

Emerald City Blues: A Novel
H. Lee Barnes

Matter Out of Place: Stories
AnnElise Hatjakes

The Stars That Fell: Poems
Gary Short

Tellin' It Like It Is: Selected Works of Adrian C. Louis
Adrian C. Louis, edited by David R. Pichaske

MATTER OUT OF PLACE

STORIES

ANNELISE HATJAKES

UNIVERSITY OF NEVADA PRESS | *Reno & Las Vegas*

University of Nevada Press | Reno, Nevada 89557 USA
www.unpress.nevada.edu

Several of these stories were previously published and are reprinted with permission: "Backscatter," *december* 33, no.1 (Spring/Summer 2022); "Alternate Route Suggested," *Bull* (March 25, 2021); "Artifacts Worth Saving," *Green Mountains Review* (February 26, 2018); "Fire Season," *phoebe* 54, no. 2 (May 15, 2025).

Manufactured in the United States of America

Cover design by Will Burrows

Library of Congress Cataloging-in-Publication Data

Names: Hatjakes, AnnElise, 1987– author
Title: Matter out of place: stories / AnnElise Hatjakes.
Other titles: Western literature and fiction series
Description: Reno, Nevada: University of Nevada Press, 2026. | Series: Western literature and fiction series | Summary: "The short story collection *Matter Out of Place* answers the question: is being from a place the same as being of it? Author AnnElise Hatjakes's writing inhabits physical and digital spaces with equal wariness, and her characters—filled with grit—navigate the fraught divide between appearances and reality."—Provided by publisher
Identifiers: LCCN 2025028693 | ISBN 9781647792299 paperback | ISBN 9781647792305 ebook
Subjects: LCGFT: Short stories
Classification: LCC PS3608.A86476 M38 2026 | DDC 813/.6—dc23/eng/20250717
LC record available at https://lccn.loc.gov/2025028693

The paper used in this book meets the requirements of American National Standard for Information Sciences—Permanence of Paper for Printed Library Materials, ANSI/NISO Z39.48-1992 (R2002).

This book has been reproduced as a digital reprint.

CONTENTS

MATTER OUT OF PLACE

1

ANDROMEDA

THE BROTHEL'S MERCH VENDING MACHINE needs restocking. That's what Sidney thinks about instead of thinking about the women lined up before her. The room's silent aside from the buzz of neon that spells *Bunny Bar* and the sounds of women adjusting their high heel straps, fluffing their hair, and straightening their sheer robes. In the next room, music plays so softly that it's hard to identify a melody; percussion so quiet it could be mistaken for her pulse.

The class that required this field trip was the easiest of the required capstone courses. At least that's what she'd told her roommate Sara. In reality, the course description thrilled her: Human Development and Family Studies 4500—Human Sexuality. The first day of class, her professor went through the syllabus in the practiced monotone of any other tenured professor, as if she wasn't describing units like "social panic and masturbation" or assignments like a sexual history narrative. Sidney hadn't had much of a sexual history herself—none that involved another person.

Her professor worms through the group until she's standing between the line of women and the shoulder-to-shoulder huddle of students.

"Thanks so much for hosting us," Professor Ludley says. The woman standing at the far-left smiles, revealing a uniform bar of white teeth. Sidney feels herself lick the front of her own teeth, crooked after two rounds of braces failed to correct the genetic memory of her father's crowded overbite. Sidney looks past the women's shoulders to see the lounge behind them. Out here in the entryway, the lights are bright enough to show mottled skin and chipped acrylic nails and loose threads dangling from lingerie. Beyond, though, it's a cave lit only by the neon and a few strings of lights that threaten to fall off the wall. At the bar, two men sit with their shoulders hitched up to their ears. This doesn't look how she expected—certainly not as frightening as her mother made it out to be, recounting the stories of two childhood friends who ended up in sex work. Lessons about loss of innocence were couched in Brothers Grimm–style fairytales with dungeons and dark magic and princesses never saved by a prince in the end.

"As I mentioned in class, you all need to turn your phones off," the professor says. She pushes her bangs away as she mouths the numbers one through ten, pointing to each of the students. She points at Trevor twice until he puts his phone away. "Liza will take it from here. Is that right?"

"That's right!" Liza says. Her voice is bright, made even brighter against the dark room they're being led into. She's wearing a purple corset and matching lace underwear. Thigh-high stockings are clipped to a garter belt, and despite Sidney's best efforts, she finds herself staring, first at Liza, then at the other women, who've disbanded and faded into the lounge.

"So, that's exactly what it'd look like for our clients when they come in," she says. "With just a little less primping." The professor nods eagerly, then looks to the students. *This is the real deal*, her nod says. It's hot in here, and Sidney wishes she could take off her coat, but she needs all three layers that separate her skin from other people's view. She imagines herself in the lineup, a tour of college students scanning her body. Their eyes might settle on the vertical scar puckering the skin on her left knee or the cluster of moles near her belly button or the mysterious rash that appeared on her chest the week before and has since begun to climb up her throat. Sidney adjusts her turtleneck.

The artwork on the walls depicts entangled bodies in minimalist lines that look like an alien language. Liza walks backward like a campus tour guide, and Sidney scans the floral carpet for unevenness. But Liza's steps are assured and comfortable; even around corners, she doesn't have to look. They're taken to what Liza calls "suite three." Sidney can't believe how unremarkable it is. A heavy oak bed and two nightstands, one topped with a heart-shaped doily. A lamp covered by a sheer red scarf. A fake fireplace.

"We have one of these buttons in every room," Liza says. It looks like a touch light, something advertised in SkyMall. "If we're ever in danger, one tap and someone will be here faster than my ex could last. And that's fast." She winks. Sidney squirms and makes a noise like laughter's preamble.

⁂

Sidney Jarette
Anya Ludley, PhD
HDFS 4500
3 March 2010

Sexual History Narrative

When I got my first period, I thought I was dying. I wrote up a will and everything, shoved all of the bloodied underwear into the back of my dresser until it took on a metallic smell. Then I changed tactics. I rolled them into fist-sized balls to fit into the fist-sized hole left by my dad in my closet's drywall. Our school had abstinence-only sex ed, a strange program that oscillated between graphic depictions of wart-laden genitalia and activities so steeped in metaphor it was hard to parse which parts were about sex. In one, you wrote your name inside a series of concentric circles—circles are the strongest shape—outlining all of the people who will be there for you if nefarious forces threaten your commitment to abstinence.

I wasn't allowed to take sex ed until it was required in high school. In seventh grade, the transfer student David (a nice kid who was rumored to have been kicked out of his Fundamentalist Church of Jesus Christ of Latter-Day Saints [FLDS] community in rural southern Nevada) and I would get pulled out and have to complete worksheets from classes we weren't enrolled in. I'd already learned about sex from my neighbor's stash of VHS pornos—a fact I've never dared share with my parents. The act seemed beastly, with cartoonishly loud moans, jerky motions, and fluids, to say nothing of the hair pulling and slapping. It seemed terrifying. For a time, I panicked whenever I heard a knock on the door. Like the man in the first video I watched, I worried one would say he was coming to fix the cable and would end up bending my mom over and pressing her face against the cold tile of our kitchen counter.

In eighth grade, I spent an entire week learning about volcanoes when I was pulled out of sex ed that year. When I got to the part about the tectonic plates rubbing up against each other—the eruption, the hot magma spilling out—my cheeks burned, my mouth dry as ash.

I understood the basics out of middle school, but it wouldn't be until much later that I experienced it for myself. Even here, in an assignment that will be read only by my professor who's read hundreds of these before, I still have trouble writing about my experience. But here it is: I had sex for the first time last week. Who the guy was is irrelevant. I didn't know him before, and I don't plan to know him after. He was good-looking in the way that a model home is appealing: uniform, predictable, nondescript. A caricature artist would have a tough time drawing him. We met at a bar where both of us were drinking, but neither of us was drunk. He invited me back to his apartment, which was one of the nice new ones near North McCarran. He drove us there. I don't remember much about the ride or the apartment or leaving. Mostly, I remember his breath, sharp with peppermint. He chewed gum the whole time and must've gone through three sticks by the time I left. And he was nervous. I remember that. His clammy hands trembled as they fumbled over the back clasp of my bra before he gave up, and the elastic snapped against my skin. At one point, he put his hand around the front half of my throat. He started to squeeze, but stopped shortly after I asked him to. Mumbled profanities when the condom fell off, some more adjusting our bodies to try to fit each other. A final effort, and then paralysis.

And then nothing.

The next morning, my roommates and I made our respective breakfasts: overnight oats for me, an energy drink and protein bar for Sara, frozen waffles for Darla.

"You got home pretty late," Sara said, cracking her energy drink open.

"Yep!" I said.

"And?" Darla asked, the word drawn out. She rubbed sleep from her eyes. "Did you go home with that weird guy?"

"Yep!" I said it loud. No chance of shame cracking through. I tried to recall what about him was weird, but nothing came up. He seemed standard issue. Nothing remarkable. Nothing memorable. The less I made my first time into a *big deal*, the less power it'd have over me. It was over. That was the most important thing. It was done and would never need to be undone or redone. I was no longer a virgin, but I hadn't *lost* anything.

"Was he any good?" Darla asked.

I shrugged. They laughed. Neither of these girls had known me when I was being pulled out of sex ed. They hadn't known me when I left my neighbor's house after watching porn and realized I was crying. I felt a jolt of pain as I stood up to wash out my jar. Neither of them seemed to notice. In the bathroom, I used the mirror of my blush palette to inspect the pain's source, but there wasn't anything unusual. The pain announced itself once in a while throughout the week that followed, but now I feel fine. It's like nothing ever happened.

Grade: 96.5/100
Submission comment:

Dear Sidney,

Thank you so much for trusting me with your narrative. I appreciate the way you were able to incorporate your writing voice and the selection of events (please see the rubric for additional feedback about the structure and style). The descriptions of your sexual education were especially compelling. I am, however, concerned about the recent incident you described, and as a mandated reporter, I may need to file a report with the Title IX office. Please come to my office hours as soon as you're able to.

Warmly,
Anya

⁂

Sjarette@unr.edu
To: aludley@unr.edu
Wed 3/10/10 6:06 pm
Subject: Submission Comment

Dear Professor Ludley,

I just read your submission comment. Thank you for reaching out, but everything is totally fine, and there's definitely no need to report anything (it was completely consensual)! On the assignment prompt, it said to "craft a narrative that demonstrates your evolving relationship with your sexuality using two to three carefully chosen events." That's what I tried to do in the assignment. I'm still feeling a little weird about what happened, but I have an appointment set up with someone in the counseling center for next week to talk more about it.

Thank you,
Sidney

⁂

Sidney's the first to ask a question during the Q&A portion of the brothel tour.

"You said that some guys, or clients, come back over and over again. Do you ever tell them anything about yourself? Like do you think they could ever find you?" She regrets the question as soon as she asks it but decides to double down. "I mean some of them are dangerous, right? That's why there are panic buttons?"

"Oh honey, no, they're not dangerous. They're lonely," Liza says. "I do tell them about myself, but only the things I want them to know. After they've been coming here for a while, I tell them my *real* name. Anything is real if someone believes it, right?" She pulls out a stick of gum that seems to materialize from nowhere. Sidney winces. "Any other questions?"

"What's the most you've ever made in one hour, do you think?" Trevor asks. Sidney's eyes dart to the professor, who glares at him. Everyone else glares at him, too. But not Liza.

"Give me your best guess," she says.

"I don't know. A thousand?" Trevor stammers.

"Try ten times that. Who was it that said they don't get out of bed for less than $10,000 a day? Well, I don't get into bed for less than $1,000."

The lounge is empty, and no one's tending bar. The professor thanks Liza, and they leave. Sidney wonders what made Liza decide on that name and whether this is her fake name or her fake real name. When she goes to the bar with her roommates that night, she realizes that there's nothing stopping her from saying she has a different name. She could be Erica or Jenny. Or maybe something more interesting. She could be Andromeda, which is both her favorite character from Greek mythology and her favorite galaxy. Sometimes called the Chained Lady, Andromeda is one of the few galaxies visible to the naked eye.

When she turns her phone back on, she has five unread texts. The most recent one says *I knew you'd ghost me.*

⁂

Sidney Jarette
Anya Ludley, PhD
HDFS 4500
10 April 2010

The Moonlite Bunny Ranch: A Herstory

The Moonlite Bunny Ranch has been publicly in operation since the early 1970s, though it was open before then in an unofficial capacity. Despite its workforce being primarily composed of women, the business has been run by men: Dennis Hof shifted from being a client to being the owner in 1992 (Hering 2006). Conspicuously absent from the history of the ranch are stories of women who work there. This might seem obvious; anonymity is often required to ensure the safety of sex workers. However, I felt it important to learn the personal history of one of the women who worked there. I was thankful that, for the purpose of this paper, our tour guide Liza sat down with me for an interview. With her permission, I have edited her responses for clarity and brevity.

Could you tell me a little bit about how you came into this line of work?

People always expect a big dramatic story, but there isn't anything that exciting about how I started working at the Ranch. No troubled childhood or anything else like that. I grew up in a small town called Ely in eastern Nevada. I played soccer in the community league and sang in the high school choir.

I took out loans for college to go to my dream school in California. I had to drop out after two years to take care of my mom when she got sick, so I left without a degree and over sixty-five grand in debt. I weighed my options, and I could either work forty-plus hours a week for a salary I could hardly live on, or I could work three days a week and make enough to live and help support my mom the other four days a week.

Can you describe the most difficult aspects of your job? The most fulfilling?

It's exhausting work, more for the emotional aspect than for the physical. I have clients who have been coming to see me for several months. They expect more and more from you each time. You'd be surprised by how many people come to see me just for the conversation. It wears on you after a while, seeing these guys who want so badly to connect with someone and haven't ever figured out how. The most fulfilling aspect is actually the other side of that same coin. I provide people with a real sense of connection. They're paying for that connection, but I make sure it doesn't feel that way when we're together.

I was struck by one of your answers during the tour about the panic button. Do you ever feel unsafe?

I feel way less safe walking down the street at night than I do at work. Men aren't all monsters, you know? Yeah, some of my clients say weird things or are more physically forceful than I'd prefer, but we're actually the ones with the power. They have to play according to the house rules—my rules—which is something I never let them forget.

Sidney responds to the text after two days, and she's not sure why. She has no interest in seeing this guy again. She doesn't want to be cruel, though. Sidney's been ghosted before. It's not the disappearance that hurts; it's the *why* that's worse than any horror movie haunting. Sidney consults her roommates before asking if he wants to meet up.

"He seemed weird, but definitely into you," Sara says. "And you're weird too."

Sidney forces a laugh. Maybe it's worth giving him a chance. It isn't going to be a meet cute like in her favorite rom-coms, but it isn't a don't-go-into-the-basement scene like in her favorite slasher movies either.

They meet up in Midtown for lunch at a gastropub that used to be a dive bar owned by a white supremacist. Shiplap covers the bathroom walls where swastikas had once been carved. Sidney asks for a table for two and realizes she doesn't really know what this guy looks like. She doesn't even have the minimal tools needed to look him up online. She repositions her silverware and tries on the sound of different names. One syllable feels right. Ben or Dan or Blake or Duke. Duke feels the most right. She drinks two glasses of water and decides that she'll give him ten more minutes before she texts him again.

Sierra Grille, right? I'm at the table in the corner.

Three minutes later, there's a man sitting in front of her, but his appearance doesn't spark any memories. This is no Duke.

"Sidney?" he says, as he sits down, unfurling the elaborately folded fabric napkin. "Sorry I'm late. Parking's gotten so bad with these new pedestrian walkways."

Sidney nods. The man flags down the waiter, who's obviously busy tending to another couple across the restaurant.

"The service here is bad. Burgers are good, though."

He flags the waiter again, and Sidney tries to express via body language—crossed arms and legs—that she's not affiliated with this man. She doesn't even know his name!

The waiter walks over, fills both of their water glasses, and asks if they're ready to put in a food order. She's not hungry anymore.

"I'll do the burger, medium well," he says. Grease darkens the roots of his light brown hair. Broken blood vessels spider around his nostrils. Despite her fixation on these characteristics, she decides that he isn't bad-looking.

"And for you?" The waiter points his pen cap at Sidney, and she apologizes.

"I haven't had a chance to look over the menu. Can you give me a minute?"

When the waiter returns, Sidney still doesn't know what to order. She asks a lot of questions. What can be taken out? What can be substituted? If she changes the options enough, she might be able to find something palatable.

"The burger's really good," the man urges. The waiter agrees. Sidney orders the burger without meat.

"I have to say that I'm surprised you responded. It didn't seem like you were interested after you left the bar with that guy."

"Oh," is all she can muster.

"You look nice. I like that sweater. What year are you?" The waiter comes by to refill their glasses, and Sidney drinks half of hers before answering.

"Thanks. It's my roommate's. I'm a junior. How about you?" She keeps scanning his face in the hopes of remembering something, anything. *That guy*, she keeps thinking. But you're *that guy*, she wants to say. When their burgers arrive, neither of them mentions that hers has meat in it, though they both notice. She pries the patty from the bun and eats a few bites before pushing her plate slightly in front of her. The man never tells her what year he is, and she realizes that he probably graduated at least ten years before. He looks to be in his mid-thirties. He tells her about his new start-up business, a software program that can help employers increase their employees' productivity by 18 percent. He tells her about growing up in a trailer park out in Sun Valley and how the principles of this program are what saved him from a life in that trailer. He calls the method 3, 2, 1. Every day, set and achieve three goals, determine two things you could improve right now, and write down one intention for the next day. It sounds exhausting. And ineffective. The waiter delivers their checks together, and Sidney snatches his so that she can see the name printed on his credit card: Alexander Eton. She's able to get a blurry picture of him as she pretends to calculate an appropriate tip.

He thanks her for lunch and walks to his car.

Is this the guy I went home with the other night???

Her roommates respond instantaneously with different versions of "no!"

In her car, she calls the Student Health Center and makes an appointment for an STI test. The pain from before has since subsided, but you can never be too safe. She deletes his contact information and shakes her head as she turns her key in the ignition. What a tool. You can't be ghosted by someone you had one conversation with at the bar.

The next weekend, she and her roommates go to the same bar. They're on a mission to find the guy she went home with. She wasn't blackout drunk that night, and she doesn't think her drink was spiked. She just doesn't remember. Her roommates aren't convinced. *He took advantage of you*, they say. They don't know that it was the other way around. She had a task to accomplish, a rite of passage to cross, a developmental stage to clear. Sara's drinking a lot of the house shot specials. They're neon green and two dollars each. She offers to beat the guy up, but Sidney assures her that's not necessary. When he walks through the door, the recognition blankets Sidney in relief. He's shorter and thinner than she remembered. Sara's attending the university on a volleyball scholarship and recently started taking jiujitsu classes. She really could beat this guy up, which is a comfort.

He gives Sidney a half wave before joining other guys at one of the corner booths. She sobers up and commits his face to memory. One of his friends calls out to him. They're up for the next beer pong game in the basement. Ben. She was right with her first guess.

Sidney considers going up to him to say something but thinks better of it. Something like hurt is in his expression when she and her roommates leave, which she relishes.

The next morning, they recount the night, ranking each other's drunkenness and assessing their dating prospects for the coming week. Darla's going on a date with a girl from her biochem lab. Sara's texting with the guy she challenged to an arm-wrestling match. Sidney's staying in. She has homework to finish.

Sidney Jarette
Anya Ludley, PhD
HDFS 4500
14 May 2010

Semester Reflection

1. Which aspects of the course did you find to be the most challenging?

I'll admit that when I chose to take this class, it was because it seemed like it'd be easy. That didn't turn out to be the case, but that's not a bad thing. There wasn't any busywork, all of the assignments were thought-provoking, and the readings were interesting.

2. What recommendations do you have for me as an instructor?

This was one of the best classes I've taken at UNR! Thank you for helping me grow and pushing me to the outer limits of my comfort zone. For students like me who have a difficult time talking about topics like this, you were very understanding. It might be helpful to be more specific about the course expectations, though. While I enjoyed doing the work, it was a very time-consuming class.

3. How do you think you've grown as a critical thinker?

As I said above, I really like the readings in this course. The one that helped me the most was the one about how women are typically the ones who do jobs that would be described as intimate labor. I've noticed that's true in my own family. My mom used to work in an assisted living facility where the only man on staff was the on-call doctor. My dad used to work at the county jail in my hometown, and I don't think he's done a moment of intimate labor in his life.

4. What surprised you the most in this course? This can refer to the materials or what you learned about yourself as a student (or just as a person)!

The field trip was the most eye-opening experience for me. When I learned that it was a required component, I almost dropped the class. In our high school, we had this group that'd come up from Vegas to *raise awareness* about how many kids are sex trafficked each year. I remember answering all of their questions, and in the end, I got a free T-shirt. It was deep red and said "Protect our kids" in cursive. It bled in the wash. The stories they told were scary—girls accepting a free cell phone and ending up trapped two states over or going on a first date only to discover the boy they'd been texting was three times their age. While I know those things do happen, I don't think my takeaways from the lesson were very helpful. They didn't let me see that people are complicated, made even more complicated by sex. As Oscar Wilde once said, "Everything in the world is about sex except sex. Sex is about power." I've been thinking about that quote a lot, especially as it relates to the excerpts from Foucault's *The History of Sexuality*. I now share his critique of the repressive hypothesis with anyone who will listen.

⁂

Sidney travels home to Tonopah, Nevada, for Thanksgiving break. Her bedroom has been transformed into what her mother calls a craft room. Her mother is now selling felt flowers and embroidered tea towels at her friend's boutique to help cover monthly expenses. Nothing else in her childhood home has changed, and both things—her changed room and the unchanged other rooms—feel like a betrayal. She helps her mother and Aunt Abigail with dinner.

"How are things up north?" her aunt asks. "Your mom was telling me that it's gotten even more dangerous. Big homeless problem there."

"No worse than any problem here," Sidney says. She turns on the hand mixer and seasons the mashed potatoes as if she knows the recipe.

Her mother and aunt exchange a look. Sidney pulls down her shirt sleeve to make sure the setting sun tattooed above the peak of her elbow isn't showing.

"Did I tell you what happened to the Jacobsen boys, Sidney?" her mother asks. She's told her the story several times and even sent the newspaper clipping from the *Pahrump Valley Times* with the only care package she ever sent.

"I think so," Sidney says with the most generosity she can summon.

"A terrible shame. How many times did I have to tell you not to play out by those mines? Their mother is just sick about it. David, the older one, will never walk right again. So much for that basketball scholarship at BYU."

David is two years younger than Sidney. When they were in high school, some kids used to drink by the abandoned mines on the outskirts of town, just beyond the Mining Park set up for tourists to visit. Sidney sends him a text, just as she had when her mother sent the newspaper clipping. That first text thread ended after she said she was sorry to hear what happened, and he thanked her for reaching out. They kissed once out by the mines. The moon had been bright, but not bright enough for them to find each other's lips on the first go. They were both a little stoned and never mentioned it again. She still thinks about him and their exile to the library during sex ed from time to time.

In the other room, Sidney's father, uncle, and two cousins sit in front of the TV. Her father grumbles as the newscaster explains that plans for a lithium mine are moving forward. The creak and pop of his recliner's footrest locking back in place, and then he's in the kitchen. He reaches over Sidney's shoulder to scoop up mashed potatoes with his pointer finger.

"Needs a little more salt," he says. "Keep up the good work, ladies." He pulls a soda from the fridge. Thanksgiving is one of the only occasions Sidney's mother allows him to drink it. He has more gray in his hair than the last time Sidney visited, but for some reason, it doesn't make him look any older. He seems happy since he retired from a thirty-five-year career at the jail. When Sidney was younger, he'd tell her any time someone local was booked. He'd say their last name and warn, "Watch out for them." David's father had been one of those people.

During dinner, the TV stays on, which Sidney is thankful for. She gives practiced responses to questions about her major and what she'll do with it after graduating. She leaves out the part about switching majors and thinking about switching minors too, from business administration to gender studies. She's the first in her family to go to college, and her parents are so proud of her. They've framed her acceptance letter and all of the Dean's List announcements her name appears on. They wouldn't be angry if she told them. Worse—they'd be scared for her. What on earth are you going to do with *that?* they'd ask.

David texts back, and they agree to meet out by the mines.

It's cold, but the sky is clear. David pulls crutches from his back seat. The brace on his left leg extends nearly to his ankle and halfway up his thigh. As they walk, she can tell it's harder for him to get around than he's letting on.

"Does it hurt?" she asks. He shrugs in between crutch swings.

"Not as bad as it did at first. A couple more months with this and then physical therapy. Should heal fine. That was one of the dumbest things I've ever done."

"We all used to do it."

"Not like this. Actually going into them. My brother started denim mining. You can get like two hundred bucks for old jeans. My flashlight's batteries went out, and we went in anyway. We knew better."

"How's he doing?"

"He's worse off than me, but he'll be fine too. My mom's making it out to be a bigger tragedy than it is. She made a website where people can donate. It's so embarrassing. I can't wait to go back to school in the spring."

They don't walk as far as they normally would before Sidney lays down the blanket. They look up at the stars, and they take turns pointing out constellations. Tonopah has some of the darkest skies; even without a telescope, you can see over seven thousand stars. Wind gusts stir sagebrush and earth, and Sidney breathes in the familiar smell. In the distant paved lot, a car parks. The headlights wink out, and Sidney feels her and David's bodies stiffen. The car soon leaves, and she relaxes back into the ground, feels her flesh contour around the hard stones pressing into her. She focuses her gaze on one star that pulsates in a slow rhythm, brightness radiating and retracting in time with her breath.

Sidney can hear that David is concealing a shiver, and she pulls a second blanket from her bag. She tucks it around both of them. Reaching for his hand, she senses the warmth of him before feeling it. They lace only their pinkie fingers. She feels a staticky jolt where they touch, as if a power line now tethers their bodies. Though clouds blow in and obstruct the sky, they still take turns guessing which stars are burning above them.

2

FIRE SEASON

EVERY SUMMER, RENO, NEVADA, AND the High Eastern Sierra foothills it's nestled within are a tinderbox. The fires are measured by the number of structures they threaten and acres they burn; they're named for the places they incinerate. Each year is the hottest year on record until the bleak honor is stolen by the year that follows.

That's why Teddy Wilson, the youngest of the three Wilson boys, should have known better than to go shooting when it was nearly one hundred degrees out. And he certainly should have known better than to shoot at an explosive cannister of Tannerite. After all, he'd gotten the idea from a news story about a gender reveal party that had ignited the 47,000-acre Sawmill Fire. Unlike those idiots, he knew what he was doing. He'd grown up doing this stuff, and his family wasn't a bunch of redneck yokels. They were claims adjusters and teachers, Eagle Scouts and PTA members who donated to the church that they didn't attend.

It seemed the fires were caused by people and lightning strikes in equal measure. No one took the drills at school seriously, even though it wasn't unusual for over a million acres to burn. Fire drills provided an opportunity for Teddy, his two brothers Jasper and Ben, and their friends to ditch school and go cool off on the banks of the Truckee River, its water choked to a creek's trickle by drought. Fires were so common that they didn't flinch when news spread about the burned-up valley, embers blown in chaotic patterns that duck, duck, goosed their way through neighborhoods, leaving one house untouched next to a house that was burned to the studs. The houses would be rebuilt using the same building plans, and sagebrush would bud, the soil more fertile in the fire's wake. May was Nevada Wildfire Awareness Month, and last year Jasper had left one of the school-sponsored presentations by a wildfire ecologist from the university knowing the degree and career he'd pursue after graduating.

Jasper will eventually be the first Wilson boy to leave Reno, taking his girlfriend and their four children to create a homestead about an hour outside of Seattle. Ben will come out after going away to college in Northern California, and though he'll know his parents will say they still love and accept him, he'll never bring the men he dates home for Christmas until he meets and marries Daniel, a sweet-hearted, clumsy Midwesterner who says *ope* when he bumps into furniture. Teddy will stick around Reno for longer than he'd hoped after he gets the young woman he meets at the bowling alley pregnant on their third date. He'll stay until the first night he's entrusted to watch the boy by himself. While he tries to prepare a bottle, the boy will roll off the couch and look dazed instead of crying. So, he'll take him to the ER, and Teddy will realize that the boy and his mother will be better served by a different, more responsible man taking his place. Then, he will be off on a soul-searching mission in the humid Southeast and rainy Pacific Northwest—anywhere by water. Finally, he'll settle down in a remote corner of Brookings, Oregon. In the last birthday card he'll send to his son—two months after his tenth birthday—he'll urge him to come to the old growth forest where he lives. He'll explain that the desert wasn't made for people to thrive in (or even survive, really) and that where he is, he can almost live off the land. He's learning how to desalinate ocean water and is building a small cabin in the branches of a redwood. He says he'll become one with nature instead of exploiting it. He will leave out the part about how Brookings is named after John E. Brookings, president of the Brookings Lumber and Box Company. In the glorified treehouse, there will be much better views than any second story apartment in Reno's Midtown. Teddy will sign off with "Love you always." When he dies in an accident while scaling a rockface on Oregon's northern coast, his son will memorialize him by taking this postcard to the tattoo shop and directing the artist to etch that phrase, written in his father's hand, into the skin stretched over his rib cage.

⁂

The Wilson boys' father had taken their mother shooting countless times when the two were dating. Your mom, Annie Oakley, he'd joke every time she tossed a piece of garbage into the can and inevitably missed by at least a foot. Dangerously, her aim was much worse when she was shooting a pistol instead of throwing an apple core into the garbage. That didn't stop them from going into the hills to shoot and taking their boys along with them when they were old enough to hold the weight of a .22 in a steady hand. The boys' shooting abilities aligned with their birth order: Jasper was a sharpshooter, Ben could usually hit the target despite having little interest in it, and Teddy wasn't much good at all. It was hard for him to forget that if a person were standing in front of the barrel, the bullet would hit them instead of the bottles lined up atop a row of lopsided fence posts.

The day of the fire was the first day back at school following summer break, and Teddy was on a date with a girl named Rose. They will be together for nearly two years—an eternity in high school romance terms—and right before they begin their junior year, she'll gently pull her hand from his during a slow skate at Roller Kingdom, leaving him as unsteady on his rollerblades as a foal just born. She'll break up with him as K-Ci and JoJo's "All My Life" plays from the speakers, and he'll stumble-roll off the rink faster than he thought his body capable. The melancholic melody won't be loud enough to conceal his guttural sobs that echo off of the bathroom's tiled walls.

Rose lived in a house one gated community over, both of their neighborhoods surrounded by saplings kept alive by steady drips of water from elaborate irrigation systems. Neither of their families would be able to afford the houses they lived in, had they bought them now instead of in 2009 when many of the foreclosed homes had been stripped of their copper pipes.

Rose had two sisters about Teddy's brothers' ages: fifteen and seventeen. He and Rose had both just started at the high school they'd gotten a variance to attend, instead of going to the school nearest them. Their mothers, who were jogging partners, had aired concerns about their children going to an underfunded school, neither of them saying that "underfunded" was a different way to say "less white."

At school, Teddy scanned each class for Rose, though he didn't know what he'd do if he saw her. When he did see her in his geography class, he imagined her in the yellow bathing suit and board shorts she'd worn at the pool that summer. It was open seating in their seventh period geography class, the announcement of which sent an electric jolt through the classroom. Rose sat next to him. The teacher was a young guy named Mr. Jennings, a self-proclaimed prankster (he will later be put on administrative leave when several parents report that he'd given their daughters wet willies when they fell asleep in class) who started the period by saying that this would be a fun class, and that fun would begin with a debate about state flags. The lyrics to the state song, "Home Means Nevada," spanned across several sheets of paper that had been laminated and posted above the white board. The classroom was hot, and the few stoners in the back had already put their hoods over their heads in preparation for a nap.

"Do you agree with that, Ted?" Mr. Jennings asked.

"Yes," he said, prompting laughter from the class, Rose included. He didn't know what he was agreeing with, but knowing Mr. Jennings, he'd probably asked if Teddy was dumb. He couldn't think about state flags, though, because he was studying the three perfectly spaced-out piercings in Rose's right ear. After class, she asked him for Jasper's number, and he gave her his own instead. He'd seen this request coming. She'd often asked whether Jasper would be dropping by the pool and watched as the boys played pickup basketball in their driveway, commenting on Jasper's height; he hardly jumped to make his layups. But the request still stung. One confusing text message exchange and some lighthearted persuasion later, Teddy and Rose agreed to a date. She had her heart set on a date with Jasper and his thick beard, but settled for Teddy and his peach fuzz, an empty promise of a beard like his brother's.

After asking for his father's permission, he got the .22 Ruger Bearcat, his father's favorite kit gun, from the safe and a handful of 40-grain bullets. He waited for Ben to leave their shared bedroom to pack the eighth of vodka Ben had stolen from the last house party they'd gone to. In the kitchen, he packed two sandwiches, which drew his brothers' and his mother's attention all the way from the adjoining living room.

"Who are you going with?" his mother asked. She pulled her hair in front of her right shoulder.

"Nobody," he said. "Did you cut your hair?"

She transferred half of her hair from the right to the left shoulder. "At least somebody noticed." She glared at their father, but the boys knew it was a joking kind of glare. Their father didn't look up from the glossy pages of a *National Geographic* issue, a rhinoceros on the cover. Their parents never got angry with each other. When his friends' parents started to get divorces, Teddy couldn't understand how such a thing was possible, having been raised by a couple whose marriage appeared to have been crafted by someone who wanted to sell people on the concept of marriage: an equal partnership with half of the bills and none of the loneliness. "That Odysseus routine isn't going to work on me."

"Rose, from down the street," he conceded. "It's not a big deal. She's never gone shooting before and wanted to try it out." His father closed the magazine.

"Make sure her parents know what you're up to. I don't want any angry calls. And be back before it starts to get dark," he said.

Teddy knew that he wouldn't do either of those things, but out of respect, he relayed his father's message to Rose when he met up with her in front of her house. She was wearing a halter top and sandals—though he was flattered that she'd changed clothes after school with him in mind, he worried that her footwear would make it hard to walk on the trail. They journeyed to the trailhead only two blocks from Rose's driveway and then made their way up the path. As soon as they transitioned from asphalt to dirt, each of their steps sent grasshoppers jumping away from their footfalls. Teddy let Rose lead the way and set their pace. He watched her calves flex as she ascended. Her steps seemed light, while his were heavy, leaving deep imprints in the dirt where she'd hardly left a trace. She stopped and turned to face him, which took him by surprise.

"Did you already do the packet for geography?" she asked.

"Not yet. That class sucks."

"I like it. It's probably going to be my easiest class. And I can tell that Mr. Jennings likes me."

They'd already been walking for at least a half hour, and Teddy realized that he had nothing to say. Why had he come out here? Why had he gone to the trouble of persuading Rose to go out with him when he was so obviously her second or maybe third choice? And why had she agreed to go along with this whole thing when she was clearly out of his league?

Instead of letting the questions linger, he allowed himself to observe and admire Rose's beauty. She was the kind of beautiful where each blemish only enhanced her appearance. The freckles across the bridge of her nose framed her eyes, and her hair's dark roots and light tips looked like they'd come from the hand of an expert stylist. Instead, both were merely evidence of the sun drawing out color through UV radiation.

"I brought food," he said, pulling out the sandwiches that had been squished by the bottle of vodka.

"I'm not hungry. Thanks, though." He wasn't hungry either, and the thought of eating peanut butter in the heat couldn't be less appealing. "I'd have some of that, though." She pointed to the bottle. His stomach twisted. Why had he brought it? He hadn't even brought water. This whole plan was unraveling.

"For sure. But I don't have any cups." They found a sole pinyon pine tree and drank from the bottle under its shade. The liquor burned, and Teddy used the PB&J as a chaser.

"Good idea," she said, laughing. Her cheeks were turning pink, and Teddy wondered if it was from the booze or the heat. "I should've worn better shoes." A thin layer of dust coated her toes. She rubbed the dust from her toenails, making the layer of shimmery purple polish brighter. The sun was starting to set. Teddy and Rose mocked two hikers who were using hiking sticks to get down the mountain's subtle slope; they were nowhere near the summit. A weak breeze rustled the brush. A lizard the size of Teddy's pinkie sunned itself on a boulder, but ran away before he had a chance to point it out. Clouds' shadows passed quickly over the ground, which made it seem like it was undulating. He picked up a twig and snapped it, picked up another one and used it to draw a circle in the dirt.

"Do you want to work on that homework together tonight?" he asked, happy to have thought of something relevant to say. This was a way to keep her around, extend their time together long enough for him to get his head right and compliment her freckles in a way that didn't sound as dumb as it did in his mind.

"No thanks. I have a study hall, so I'll probably do it then." Her voice was gentle. She wrapped her arms around her knees. "Maybe we can work together for that group project, though."

"Here, you'll love this." Teddy pulled out the Bearcat and plastic container of Tannerite. He set it up on a teal floral couch someone had dumped in the ravine nearby. Couches, washing machines, and bags of trash from home renovations littered this part of the mountain, where people could dump what they wanted to without having to pay a nickel to Waste Management. More than once, he'd seen people dump their furniture from trucks that often had a bumper sticker warning, "Don't Tread on Me" in letters being crushed between a rattler's unhinged jaws. He could feel himself sweating and wished he'd asked the hikers for some water. The peanut butter stuck to his gums, making it hard to wrap his lips around his teeth. And the vodka made it even harder to wrap his lips around any words. He looked back at her to make sure she was watching from her spot several yards back.

"Do you want to do it?" Teddy called out, a slight echo bouncing back to him.

"No, do you want to?" Rose asked. "You're going to shoot it? What are you doing?" Teddy couldn't tell if he was understanding her questions in the opposite order that she was asking them, or if she was really asking them in that order.

"I'll shoot it. Watch." Teddy stood closer to the target than he normally would if he weren't so off balance. If his parents were here, they would be disappointed. They trusted him enough to give him the keys to the safe, and he'd broken that trust. And for what?

He shut one eye knowing that it wouldn't improve his aim and shot three times before a bullet connected with the Tannerite. The explosion was louder and bigger than he expected, blanketing at least a ten-foot radius of sagebrush in pink. There was a faint hum in his ears, and he knocked his palm against his temple as if doing so would knock the sound out of his head.

Rose clapped from her spot under the tree. Teddy carefully emptied the chamber and put the safety on, as if to un-disappoint his parents in his imagined scenario of them watching him from behind the brush.

Teddy sat down next to Rose, and she looked like she might kiss him, but instead she wrapped her arm around his shoulder and requested he carry her back home.

"It's just my shoes," she said. She pointed at them by way of explanation. As soon as he picked her up, he saw that black-gray smoke was filling the air that had been a pink haze just moments before.

And then there was fire. Everywhere. Teddy put Rose down. He texted Jasper, begging him to pick them up, and his brothers were there within a few minutes. In the truck, they watched the fire advance across the hillside, the line of flames and embers marching in a blood orange line. Jasper drove their pickup down the hill faster than the two-wheel drive Toyota could handle. The dust was nearly settled by the time they'd finished winding down the dirt path pocked with holes from smaller, kicked up boulders. They bounced in unison, packed tight into the truck's extended cab. A garden shovel, a bottle of weedkiller, and some loose soil rolled within the truck bed's grooves, taunting the boys for not completing the gardening project they were supposed to be working on as a gift for their mother's birthday—yellow poppies planted in the shape of a heart in their side yard. They'll later finish the project just in time, but like all non-native flowers planted in the Orovada soil, these will crumple before dying of thirst.

The fire moved so quickly and effortlessly that for a moment Teddy thought it a cleansing force, and imagined the flames incinerating the Styrofoam cups and the floral couch. Through the roar and distant sirens, he thought he heard the pop of glass from the eighth of vodka he'd left behind.

"What were you thinking?" Ben asked in between a distant fire engine's wail.

"I don't know." This was an honest answer. He scanned his memory for the thoughts that immediately preceded the shot and realized that he might have been thinking about Rose's freckles. He looked at her now, and she was shivering despite the heat. "It was an accident."

"You smell like booze," Jasper said, downshifting as they turned out from the trailhead. Rose's eyes were on Jasper. Teddy maneuvered closer to her.

"No, I don't," he said, pursing his lips.

"Dad's going to flip his shit," Ben said in an even tone. He was stating the facts, something that he did often, usually highlighting facts that leaned toward the nihilistic. Everyone dies, there is no God, Dad's going to flip his shit.

They dropped off Rose. She bent over to clean whatever dust she could by patting and wiping her clothes and legs. They could all see the smoke from her driveway. More wails from the firetrucks.

"You okay?" Jasper asked as Teddy crawled out of the narrow cab to permit her exit.

"I'm fine," she said. "I'll see you tomorrow?" She walked inside before hearing a response. She was shaken, but the steadiness of her voice made Teddy forget what he'd done for one moment; it felt like the one bright star in an otherwise inky night sky.

At home, Teddy reported what happened quickly, leaving out many key details and relying heavily on passive voice. A fire was started. 911 was called. Ben and Jasper stood next to Teddy with their arms crossed as if standing guard, bouncers who would intervene if needed. But their parents didn't yell. It was worse than that. Their father said he was disappointed, looked to be on the brink of tears. Their mother didn't say anything. Teddy felt like his words had stopped short of her, like they were still hanging in the air and she hadn't chosen to gather them. She hugged Teddy then, and gently rocked him. He sobbed and his body shook. The more it shook, the harder she squeezed.

Like that summer, the early fall will also suffer record-breaking temperatures, and the Wilsons will shake their heads as they watch the news when the weatherman notes the historic highs. They'll say that, personally, they're thankful that at least it's not fire season anymore, no school closures due to poor air quality and falling ash. And when Teddy is eventually charged for instigating the fire, his mother will be defiant. She will accuse them of using a teenager as a scapegoat for a natural disaster. And Teddy will hear the conviction in his mother's voice, a warming reassurance that he will eventually believe is true. Since he is a minor and it truly was an accident, he will get off with a very stern warning, a big fine, and a lot of community service. Rose's name will never be mentioned. Her parents will threaten to make her go to the school she's zoned for the following year, arguing that there are too many bad influences at her high school. Though they won't follow through, the threat of separation will feel Montague and Capulet romantic, and it will actually bring Teddy and Rose together again to seal their fate as high school sweethearts.

Teddy will feel guilty for what he's done and will think it's unfair that the evidence of his mistake is so visible. Eventually, though, during a sloshy, bar-hopping period of his thirties, the story will serve as currency, which he'll expertly trade for the rapt attention of other patrons. The story will take on new elements, the truth stretched to its limits, right up until he can see skepticism furrow his audience's brows and the story snaps back to its original shape.

His son will grow up hearing this story, as told by his mother. It will take on a fairytale quality. The boy who burned down a mountain just to impress a girl. It will take years for anything to grow enough to cover the layers of ash on Peavine Mountain. And by the time that it returns to a version of its pre-fire self, Teddy's son, now twenty-six, will be hiking up that same mountain, nervous as he prepares to propose to his girlfriend of two years. He will unfold a blanket when they reach the peak and sweep away any brush and pebbles that would be uncomfortable to sit on. After he sets up the picnic of a prepackaged charcuterie board and sparkling wine, he'll pause before standing up. She'll turn around to see him on one knee and put her hands over her mouth, behind which she'll whisper, *oh my god.* They'll embrace before she says yes, and they'll look over the city. The ring on her finger, a fire opal from the Royal Peacock Opal Mine in Denio set in a thick gold band, will take a while to get used to. Eventually, though, she won't be able to imagine her finger without it, and during her two pregnancies, the flesh of her finger will grow wider, trapping the ring in place. When she is put in the Sierra Assisted Living Facility at 82, she'll still stare into the ring, an entire galaxy contained in the electric blue and orange speckles on the stone's face.

The newly engaged couple will see the cluster of casinos downtown and the vast stretch of uninhabited land to the west and talk about carving out their own place in the desert, somewhere close to the water that cuts through it.

3

BACKSCATTER

MAYA'S SOON-TO-BE EX-HUSBAND, JOHN, HAS been born again. His new girlfriend tagged him in a typo-riddled transcription of Romans 10:9. Maya shook her head as she scrolled past the post, returned to it, clicked through his girlfriend's photos, scrolled past it again. She tossed her phone onto the other queen bed in her hotel room and turned on the TV.

John had asked for one day to box up and clear out his things, and Maya decided to treat herself to a night in a hotel with room service and cable, wrap herself up in a blanket of nostalgia for times when hotel stays meant impromptu vacations, and not trips back to her hometown for distant family members' funerals or professional development conferences in Phoenix.

At first, in between bites of cold French fries and swallows of white wine, she made jokes in her head about a ghost hunting show called *Paranormal Mysteries*, then laughed. A one-woman performance for a one-woman audience. Yes, that door closed completely on its own, and not thanks to the production intern. Oh, 6.5 mg on the electromagnetic field meter, you say? Must mean there are ghosts lurking in every corner!

But soon, she felt invested in each of the stories of these rooms' hauntings, started to multitask with her media consumption, the show on TV and news articles about paranormal sightings on her phone during commercial breaks. They were playing a 24-hour ghost-a-thon, and she'd watched as much of it as she could stay awake for.

Maya ordered another bottle of wine, ignoring the judgmental tone of the concierge's voice as she did so. The cheap screw-top bottle was delivered on ice, but it was still room temperature. Distracted by a story about a five-year-old child named Elliot who was murdered and then stowed in a crawl space, she spilled some of her wine as she poured it into the tumbler. She sopped the spill up using the pile of tissues she'd been crying into earlier.

By the third episode, she felt that she understood the ghost hunting duo's routine and dynamics. Boris was a parapsychologist who, prompted by his own brush with death following a hang-gliding accident, studied what happened in the liminal space between life and death. He never really reacted to potential sightings, and in the night vision recordings, Maya thought he was oddly attractive. In contrast to Boris, Patricia always screamed and asked ridiculous questions that seemed scripted at first, but that slowly began to seem more earnest. She didn't have as clear of a specialty as Boris did. In one confessional, though, she said that she had been sensitive to paranormal activity since she was a young girl. She often played hide-and-seek with her dead aunt and grandmother. No one believed her until she attended a taping of *The Montel Williams Show*. The psychic Sylvia Browne had a segment on that episode, and Patricia had the rare fortune of being selected for a reading. Sylvia flubbed two of the responses to Patricia's questions about her dead aunt. Following Patricia's assertion that Sylvia was wrong (Patricia had confided in her aunt that very morning), she ended up being invited on stage to perform a reading for a fellow audience member who wished to contact her deceased dog.

Maya applied a hydrating sheet mask to her face and avoided

catching a glimpse of her own ghoulish appearance in the mirror near the TV by repositioning herself on the bed. She watched another episode of *Paranormal Mysteries*, which was set in an abandoned orphanage in rural Michigan. In it, the paranormal detectives took out their equipment and began to measure the electromagnetic levels in the room. Maya froze, glass positioned halfway between her lap and her lips, when she heard a quiet scraping.

"Did they hear that? Get out the recorder," Maya instructed. She clicked up the volume until the scraping was deafening. "How are they not using the EVP recorder?" Patricia yelled out that she saw something, and her voice was so loud that Maya nearly jumped out of her bed. She frantically turned down the volume and hoped that whoever was in the next room wasn't startled by the sound, and—more importantly—that they didn't recognize which TV show she was watching.

Later that night, she began scrolling through product reviews of paranormal toolkits for beginners on her phone. The familiar anxiety of John criticizing her for another package on the front steps hardened in her gut, and then dissolved. He would not be there to ask what was in the box this time. She imagined what would await her when she returned to her house. What would he deem essential, and which remnants of their life together would he leave for her? She hoped John would return the few remaining unwrapped, but unopened, gifts from their baby shower before she got back, and before the 90-day return policies took effect. It would be a small but important kindness, which was the only type of kindness he was any good at showing.

Following the death of their daughter, 186 hours after her birth, the two traveled in opposite directions. John found God, while Maya purposefully lost any holdovers of Him from her Lutheran upbringing. Their daughter was named for Maya's grandmother,

Mary, and she'd been born with a severe atrial septal defect. When Maya and John pleaded for a clearer explanation of what that meant, the doctor said that Mary had an inoperable hole in her heart.

Maya found that desperately poetic now.

She joined the Paranormal Society of Nevada Facebook group, revisited John's girlfriend's page one more time, and changed her profile picture to one of her posing with her arm wrapped around a statue of Mark Twain. The sleek silhouette of her pre-baby body fitted into a black cocktail dress stood out in contrast to Twain's lumpy suit cast in bronze. Then, she curated her profile, deleting old pictures and unfriending John's relatives and friends who'd sided with him after the divorce. She imagined herself the executor of her own will as she generously bequeathed many of their shared friends to John.

Maya set the TV's sleep timer for an hour and surrounded herself with the pillows from the other queen bed so that she was enveloped in a bedding cocoon. As she slept, ghosts and scraping sounds permeated her dreams, and she awoke to a woozy loneliness.

Nearly a year after the divorce was finalized, Maya decided to start dating again. Months of hints, suggestions, and outright directives to get back out there from the people who loved her had worn her down. She met up with a fellow member of the paranormal group named Ellory, a man who was in his late forties, at least fifteen years her senior. He was sweet and vulnerable, unafraid to send her a video of him singing off-key to the strum of his guitar. His song, titled "Apparitions," had been inspired by a photo of his father standing with his hands on his hips, a faded white orb floating above his head. Maya had studied photography before committing to an accounting track, but resisted the urge to tell him that the orb was only backscatter; the camera's lens or the room itself needed cleaning.

The Electronic Voice Phenomena recordings and Electromagnetic Field Meter readings—those made sense, were at least a little supported by scientific reasoning. The orbs didn't. She would keep this to herself, though. Ellory liked her. When they talked on the phone, he laughed heartily at her jokes, even the ones constructed with minimal effort.

They met for coffee at a hip coffeeshop that was all subway tile and Edison lightbulbs, and as they ordered their drinks, both of their hands shook for different reasons. They suffered through conversational false starts, accidentally talking over one another, both saying different forms of, "No, you go first." He pulled the picture that had inspired his song from his wallet. It was smaller than it looked in the version he'd sent her online.

"Here's what got me started with all this. See it there." He aggressively fingered the orb above his father as if identifying a suspect in a lineup. "We think it's my grandfather who died in that same bedroom where this was taken. Isn't that something?"

Maya nodded. To keep from having to respond, she continued drinking despite the liquid's burn on her lips.

"My ex-wife was afraid of paranormal activity, but I'm not. I blame the media, horror movies and all that. It's a very egotistical view to think that out of the millions of people who've died and the thousands of years humans have been around, ours is the only energy that's allowed to stick around, don't you think?"

Maya suddenly recalled the sloshy rhythm of her daughter's heartbeat—a metronome at the bottom of a lake—during the first ultrasound and the feeling of cold jelly spreading across her stomach. The shaking of her hands intensified, but the liquid in her cup held steady.

She nodded again.

"What kind of camera was used to take the picture?" she asked, quickly adding, "Just curious."

Ellory knit his brows and shrugged in consideration of and answer to her question. She'd read that a point-and-shoot camera was just as good as a DSLR to capture photographic evidence of spirits, but she didn't believe it.

The clatter of mugs on saucers as someone bussed a nearby table startled Maya more than it had any right to. This was not just jitteriness, but alertness, which was a new development. After her paranormal investigation equipment came in the mail, she'd measured the levels in her house and scoured available death disclosure records. Nothing out of the ordinary, but even so, she'd started to feel hyperaware of the energy around her. Every time the swamp cooler sucked in air or the house settled into its foundation, she imagined it yawning and lying down for a rest. She'd read that this was to be expected. Becoming aware of human energy fields made it seem like everyday objects were coming to life.

"Shall we?" He offered her his hand as if she needed help standing up, a gesture that irked and delighted her at the same time. He dropped another two dollars into the tip jar before they left and thanked the barista for the drinks. John never would have done this. He often complained about the service and the prices here. When she'd order her usual vanilla latte, he'd always raise his eyebrows in feigned disbelief after the price was announced. He'd order a black coffee and joke that if she needed all that milk and sweetener in her coffee to make it palatable, she might not like coffee.

Ellory asked if she'd like to go for a walk, and she agreed.

"I have a special place I want to show you," he said as he quickened his pace. They walked through a park that felt like a placeholder for something else. She could wrap her hand around the trunks of the brand-new trees planted there, and the freshly laid sod still had visible seams between the rectangular patches. As they walked along the asphalt footpath, a man sitting at the edge of his stool offered to draw their caricature, and the two gave opposite responses. Maya knew which of her facial features would be caricatured. Her mother used to say she had big puppy dog eyes, but she later discovered this was actually a symptom of hyperthyroidism. After Mary died, the doctor said that what happened to her was not a product of Maya's condition, but John's own research revealed otherwise.

"It'll be fun!" Ellory pressed, and she agreed. He sat up straight and smiled wide as the artist drew, while Maya tried to maintain a pleasantly neutral expression. The sketch only took about ten minutes to produce. Ellory laughed at the image that was presented to them, which didn't seem to offend the artist as he took a crisp twenty-dollar bill from Ellory's hand. The drawing didn't capture him at all, but the big eyes of Maya's two-dimensional double looked just like hers. Thankfully, Ellory folded the sketch in half and then in quarters before stowing it in his inside blazer pocket.

"I'll keep it close to my heart," he joked, and she gave a half-hearted laugh.

They continued walking for at least another two miles before approaching another park. She rarely came to this part of Reno, which featured a bizarre combination of industrial buildings and pastures for cattle. The park where they stopped this time was more well-established than the first. The trees rooted here looked like they belonged. Maya wondered how many people these trees had already outlived and how many more they would outlive in the future. She almost said this to Ellory, but decided against it. Since beginning her paranormal research, she thought about death frequently, but these thoughts weren't dark or scary. They were the kinds of philosophical musings she might have shared with her college roommate when they were stoned. She wondered how many of the leaves rustling and birds chirping were actually messages from another realm. And why every culture somehow independently conceived of similar stories to explain death and life after death. And if the dead dreamed of the living like the living did of the dead.

Ellory put his arm around her shoulder, and their joint movements were more fluid than she anticipated. The heat from his body warmed her and made her realize that she felt cold.

It wasn't until they neared the park's edge that she realized they were not in another park. They were in a well-maintained cemetery. She instinctively checked her phone to see if any paranormal presence might have sapped her battery.

Maya could feel Ellory observing her, so she quickly put her phone away and apologized.

"This is where my family's plot is," he said, unfazed. Maya knew she should feel strange about where her date had taken her, that she should leave and never call him again, that this might be a funny "told you so" story to tell the people who urged her to date. But instead, she began reading the names on the headstones and doing the math to calculate their ages. "I hope you don't think this is too weird, but I wanted to see what you thought about the energy here."

Now that he mentioned it, she did feel something about the energy, but she couldn't tell if it was coming from Ellory or from the ground he stood on. She knelt down and pressed her hand into the grass, waiting for someone's presence to come up and weave its way in between her fingers. But all she felt was the prick of a bull thistle's leaves.

⁂

Maya had planned to do her first on-site investigation by herself, using her own equipment and the techniques she'd taught herself, drawing her own conclusions. But when Ellory asked if she wanted to go with him and a small group two weeks after their first date, she said yes before really turning the idea over in her mind. After measuring the base levels of her house, she'd stored everything away. She was protecting herself from unpredictable, and potentially unfavorable, outcomes, just as she did whenever she was sick, and refused to go to the doctor who'd confirm that sickness with his pen's permanent ink on her chart.

Based on her research, Maya knew to keep her expectations low. These group investigations were not as dramatic as they seemed in the movies, or even on the TV shows she'd binged. She might see flashes of light, some EMF spikes, might hit a cold spot if she was lucky.

The group had chosen to do their investigation in Virginia City, an old mining town turned tourist trap. The windy 45-minute drive was quiet until Ellory turned on staticky talk radio and reacted to the news headlines as they were delivered. At one point, he rested his hand palm up on the center console, which she took as an invitation. She rested her hand in his until both began to sweat. They met up with the other three investigators in front of the Bucket of Blood Saloon, and Maya jumped at the bang of a cap gun, which made the boy holding it laugh. His mother shushed him and warned that she would take it away if he shot it one more time before they got home.

"Are you okay?" Ellory reached for Maya, and she recoiled. "I think you might be sensitive like me. Extra sensory perception."

"No, I'm not. I've just been jumpy lately." She did suspect that she might be sensitive, but wasn't ready to tell anyone this; to say so out loud might make it real, transform this hobby into a belief. When she was younger, her mother spanked her when she blamed broken vases and missing cookies on an imaginary friend named

Kitties. Now that she looked back, she couldn't remember whether she'd actually seen someone, or if she'd just grown accustomed to the attention from saying she did.

John had taken Maya to Virginia City on one of their first dates. She'd recently moved to Reno for a job at the accounting firm where she still worked. John had grown up here. He'd described Virginia City as "cheesy as hell," but she genuinely liked the town the moment they set foot on the sidewalks composed of uneven wooden planks. They'd laughed at a group of investigators just like the one she was now a part of. But they were young, drunk on whiskey served out of jugs marked xxx, unable to think of any possibilities not explained by a thirty-second search online. They'd taken old-timey photos in sepia tone, him pointing two pistols in the air and her wearing fishnets, a corset, and a feather boa. Where was that photo? Had he taken it with him when he left?

Ellory shot a knowing glance. "I remember how strange everything seemed during my first investigation here. It fades away with time." Maya thought of the condolence cards she received while she was still in the hospital, many of them bearing some version of the assurance that time would heal all wounds.

Everyone introduced themselves and their fields of expertise as they checked out each other's equipment. Maya planned to talk to the demonologist, a woman with wispy brown hair and alternating gold and silver rings on each finger, after the investigation.

Something about the group disconcerted her. It may have been the fact that they all looked related somehow, all of them sprouted from the outer spindly limbs of one family tree. Maya was the youngest, and though she was here too, she resented the fact that none of these other people had anything better to do on a Saturday. Seeing a couple pose with a man costumed like a nineteenth-century drunk in a mining town—red long johns, white beard, and well-worn black Boss of the Plains hat—and his donkey made the heat of embarrassment redden her cheeks. She quickly packed up her gear, and while they all walked through the Washoe Club, she avoided making eye contact with any of the bar's patrons.

Before they descended into the crypt, the demonologist asked if they would like her to lead a prayer. Maya was the only one who said no, so the woman proceeded. Everyone cast their equipment aside to either fold their arms or clasp their hands in front of them. Ellory nodded at Maya before following suit.

"We ask that all negative thought forms, residues, elementals, lost souls, and fragments be permanently healed and taken into the light, that all may be freed according to the highest will of God," she said, prompting a quiet chorus of amens, Maya's amen the quietest.

The group had agreed not to hire a guide and had done their research independently, each offering their own collected information as they walked. After turning on her EMF and EVP recorder, Maya explained that this was where deceased miners were stored during the winters when the ground was too hard to bury them. One of the hunters turned on his headlamp, and Maya saw his nod in the moving beam of light on the wall adjacent to her. The air was cold and damp, but she took off her sweater anyway so that she could feel any cold spot that the thermographic camera might not pick up. The demonologist shivered, which Maya took to be a good sign, but then she explained that she was getting over the flu.

They left after an hour of recording their meters, which remained unchanged. The demonologist said a closing prayer: "Spirits of light, we appreciate and thank you for your time and wisdom." Maya said her own silent prayer that all souls found peace.

As night fell, they walked to the Silver Queen Hotel, which held more promise, having been described on the website as a "ghost hunter's delight." Too drunk to make the windy drive home, Maya and John had stayed at this hotel on their date, and now the same kind-eyed woman who'd checked them in was seated at the front desk. Thankfully, the woman did not seem to recognize Maya as Ellory explained that the group was going to see room eleven.

"Let me know if she pays you a visit," the woman said cheerfully.

"This room is frequently visited by the spirit of a prostitute named Rosie," Ellory explained as he unlocked the door. "She died in this hotel, and several staff members have confirmed her presence here."

"She killed herself," another man added. Maya already knew this, which was why she was walking toward the bathtub where the suicide was believed to have happened. She felt the energy change immediately. The space felt surreal, as if they'd become playthings in a giant's dollhouse. She felt the gentle throb of her pulse and heard a light ringing in her ears. Her heightened awareness helped her pick the perfect spot to set up right next to a vanity. She took off her sweater and draped it over the mirror since her heat sensor could potentially pick up on its reflection.

"I've got something over here," she said, louder than she meant to. The other four people rushed over and watched the needle of Maya's EMF meter bounce wildly. Ellory grabbed a camera from his bag to record the phenomenon. Someone's phone started to buzz in their pocket.

"Sorry. My daughter keeps calling," another group member said. "Trying to set up a time to see the grandkids." Maya shushed him. As soon as he turned off his phone, the needle stopped moving and everyone filtered out of the cramped enclave that housed the clawfoot tub.

"False alarm," Ellory said. Maya scowled at him.

"This isn't affected by cell phones. They don't produce anywhere near the same frequency," she explained, gesturing for Ellory and the rest of the group to return to the spot near the tub. Ellory put his hand on her shoulder and again asked if she was okay. She was not making this up. She knew how to read her equipment and how to watch out for signs of matrixing or pareidolia. Some of the other hunters might choose to see a familiar pattern where one did not exist, but she didn't. The ringing in her ears intensified, and the tension in her limbs went lax. She heard a woman comforting a crying child. Did Rosie have a child? She looked to Ellory to see if he heard the same.

But when she looked into his eyes, she saw something that she hated, something in the space between sympathy and pity. So many people had asked her if she was okay in the last year and a half. She'd lost count after the first two weeks. They asked her in order to alleviate their own discomfort from seeing her hollowed out cheeks and the gray half-moons set beneath her eyes. Of course she was not okay, but that was not a polite admission to make. It was not polite to worry people, make your mother feel like she has to check in every afternoon, make your husband act as the first line of defense against reminders of the baby, make acquaintances feel compelled to deliver casseroles.

Better every day, she'd lie.

"No," she mumbled and didn't pack up her equipment before leaving the room. Ellory and the rest of the group might make better use of it. The stairs were uneven, as were her steps. The staircase felt hotter during her descent than it had during the ascent, and she struggled to get air. It was as if someone had lit a fire that snatched all of the oxygen from the corridor.

She got her breath back after escaping from the narrow stairwell and sitting on the final step. A tourist group edged toward her, their guide explaining the Silver Queen portrait's origin story, how over 3,000 Morgan silver dollars had come to be arranged atop the painting. They all stared at Maya instead of the portrait as they walked. One woman even appeared to be taking a video.

"Room 11?" the guide asked. Maya nodded, knowing that these people needed something to believe. They shuffled past her, eyes wide with anticipation.

Before leaving, she took in the portrait of the Silver Queen, who watched hundreds of visitors as they came and went. Despite the thousands of silver dollars inlaid in the queen's dress, the portrait didn't reflect any light. Instead, the woman seemed to be sinking into the black brushstrokes that shadowed her. Maya wondered what this city looked like when it was a booming metropolis. Before there were men in red long johns posing for photos, there was the single largest deposit of silver in America. What had they lost when the silver ran out?

4

HORSEPLAY

You can be anyone you want at Burning Man, so Willow decided her first year that she was going to be like the attendees she'd put on her Wanderlust Vision Board: beautiful women who, like her, were in their early twenties, but who, unlike her, seemed to *get it*. They knew what to wear and how to act without strategizing or researching. They wore fishnet one-pieces, metallic gold fanny packs, and Victorian-era gowns, traipsed across the desert in apocalyptic glamour. They posed for photos that seemed simultaneously planned and candid where they shyly looked over their shoulders, sat cross-legged on the ground, and stood with hands extended into the air. They were in their element.

Day two of her experience, and Willow was not in her element. She was a transplant to a small town, an undercover cop, a cultural anthropologist who observed customs without participating in them. It took a few hours of leafing through the Burning Man guide she'd printed to get up the courage to leave her camp.

Willow climbed up to the second story of an art car shaped like a squid. Like the other sculptures on wheels roaming the playa, this one represented an artist's vision at the intersection of form and function. She pictured welding masks and calloused fingers, metal sheets and bolt cutters.

The DJ blasted techno music that overtook the normally silent playa; rhythmic bass and sampled reggae melodies boomed across the Black Rock Desert where trees and buildings weren't there to obstruct the sounds' travel. The DJ's white guy dreads hung down to the studded belt that wasn't doing much to hold up his cutoff cargo pants. When he turned and she saw his face, her surprise that he was hot—chiseled cheek bones and a dimpled superhero chin—inspired a tiny crush. Crushes come easily when you're partying at 11 a.m. on a squid car. Anything really could happen. What *did* happen stamped her crush straight out: he wrapped his arm around a woman whose body looked like the ones plastered on Willow's vision board.

The DJ and the perfect woman started to make out, and a string of saliva connected them after they'd parted. Willow realized that in addition to controlling the music, he was also controlling the art car's pyrotechnics. Flames blew from the squid's head, prompting cheers from the people around her. Someone offered her a drink of water from a canteen strapped across his chest and enthusiastically nodded to the beat, as if to remind Willow that it was customary to dance when loud music was playing. Willow danced halfheartedly, but she couldn't bring herself to unfold her arms, which were crossed over her stomach.

From the top of the art car, she could almost make out her camp on B street, this year named Breath. She could also see the women participating in the Critical Tits Parade, which helped her to understand why her ex-boyfriend said that you stop noticing the nudity after a while. The parade was composed of hundreds of topless women. Some modest types wore pasties that covered their nipples, while others' chests were adorned only with swimsuit tan lines. She winced at the imagined sensation of sunburned nipples. She watched the sea of moving body parts contained by banks of supportive spectators. A man yelled out "You're all beautiful!"

Willow hadn't packed her glasses or her contacts, so she strained to finally find the rod topped with a Christmas tree angel that marked her neighbor's camp. As she walked toward it, she adjusted her tutu, sequined bikini top, and feather boa. She'd learned too late that burners frowned on feather boas that came apart and littered their bright traces—or MOOP—all over the playa.

Her skin was burning, and she tried to find a shade structure to protect herself. The alkali dust that'd collected on her skin during the last dust storm offered a small amount of protection. She found a bar called Heaven, where she reapplied sunscreen she'd bummed from a friendly lady who had the patient expression of an overworked kindergarten teacher. The woman wore a tin cup wrapped with gold foil around her neck so that she didn't have to rely on disposable cups. Light bounced off one of the many disco balls, hitting the tin cup and returning again.

"Smart," Willow whispered. She'd make something like that the next time she came.

"Great minds," the woman said, pointing to her shirt and then to Willow. The baggy T-shirt was printed with the form of a bikini-clad woman. One of the bartenders overheard and laughed to fill the pause between the woman's joke and Willow's understanding of it. From behind a cloud-shaped bar, he generously poured gin into the woman's necklace cup. They got so close that Willow thought they might kiss.

"Don't get burned," the woman said, cheers-ing Willow's empty water bottle as she stumbled from the tent. Fans equipped with misters were hung up around the tent, but they did little to cool the air; water couldn't travel far before evaporating. Once-white beanbags lined the ground, and Willow wedged herself in between two of them. She kept expecting someone to strike up a conversation with her, ask her where she was from, what she did when she was in the Default World. No one approached her, though. They were engaged in their own conversations, only acknowledging her every once in a while with what she interpreted to be suspicion. *Undercover cop who doesn't drink. Cultural anthropologist who doesn't get the local humor. Normie spy.*

Willow decided to make her way out to deep playa to take some photos of the art, some other photos of herself in front of the art. These pictures would help her do what she'd come here to do, though she did not fully articulate that purpose to anyone, including herself: make her ex jealous and put together a modeling portfolio. People were always telling her that she should model, but this suggestion often followed a hard-edged compliment. "You have such a unique face shape" or "I've never met anyone with gray eyes before" or "You've finally grown into your features."

She wished her younger sister, Juniper, was there to reassure her that her outfit was cute. But she was alone. She hadn't even bought a ticket. Instead, she'd found someone on Craigslist who was selling a work access pass they'd likely salvaged in nearby Gerlach that granted in-and-out privileges, for $100. She'd had to mend it back together using fishing line.

A dust storm kicked up as she walked out to deep playa. There'd been more dust storms this year than any others—a conviction held by Burning Man virgins like Willow every year. She attempted to unzip her Hello Kitty backpack, but the zipper's teeth were gummed up with dust. After some struggle, she opened the bag and pulled out her goggles. They hardly improved her ability to see through the dust. Walking through the storm made her feel like she was on an alien planet, a feeling that was intensified by the sight of a woman walking on stilts who seemed to apparate from a dust devil. Willow didn't want to risk getting lost without any landmarks in sight, so she sat down on the ground and focused on the small crevasses formed by dryness cracking it open. She'd researched all of the wrong things for this trip. Instead of researching what to pack and how to keep dust out of her tent, she'd researched the history of the place, the land that she'd drive her camp stakes into. She read that the Black Rock Desert playa spans almost 200 squares miles and is known for its resilient ecosystem made to thrive in the arid conditions. Tracing the cracks, Willow imagined what Lake Lahontan had looked like 15,000 years ago, before revelers gathered to share and celebrate art. She identified shapes in the ground like she and her ex-boyfriend often did with clouds in the sky. There, a ballerina. And there, a star cut at jagged angles.

The dust settled after a few minutes, but it felt much longer. The playa skewed and warped time. Few people wore watches. When Willow had asked someone what the time was earlier, he'd looked at his bare wrist and said, "It's a quarter past a freckle."

In the surrounding hummocks and dunes, you could find kit foxes and rattlesnakes. Not here, though. Here in deep playa, it was only Willow and a kinetic sculpture of a wild horse made from scrap metal. Like the woman from before, it suddenly appeared through the constant swirl of dust. The horse's slow gallop was powered by the breeze. Later, Willow would learn that the sculpture's eyes lit up red at night. The creator, a woman who taught financial literacy at Truckee Meadows Community College, called the piece "Horseplay." Willow tried to climb on the horse to take a picture (it appeared to be one of the interactive pieces), but before she could get into its saddle, she felt a tug on her inner thigh.

The pain didn't hit until she saw blood.

Twin paths of blood traveled down from her leg, instantly drying into semipermanent streaks. It was a throbbing pain, not sharp like she imagined a cut from rebar would be. She took a picture of the wound and brainstormed captions for when she got cell service again and could post it. She then adjusted her modest cleavage in her bikini top and posed in front of the offending sculpture; one big thumbs down and a frown, along with the picture of the sculpture, would tell an entire story.

The bleeding didn't stop, so Willow found her way to one of the emergency service stations. After walking all the way back, she could feel blisters bubbling up on the soles of her feet. She would've asked for help with the blisters too, but worried that these were yet another sign of her lack of preparation. Willow squeezed through the tent's narrow opening. Inside, it looked like an actual hospital —not like the flimsy two-person tent she'd set up.

"Excuse me. Could I get a bandage please?" she asked. Four people looked up at her in unison.

"Oh sweetie, let's get you cleaned up," one of them—the only woman—said.

"Where are you camped?"

"I'm on B."

"Want us to send for someone there?" The woman put on latex gloves and opened up a plastic case, unspooled some gauze. "We don't have pads here, but this should hold you over until you get back to camp."

Willow froze. The three men made themselves look busy. Thankfully, someone who'd gotten too drunk and was dehydrated redirected their attention. Willow had heard so much about the wild parties and the drugs that she was surprised when the only people who seemed to be causing problems were legally pursuing their altered states of mind.

"Oh no. It's not my period." She pulled up her tutu, revealed the flap of skin cut into a crescent.

The woman rubbed Willow's shoulder.

"I see. I see. I'll get you fixed up." The woman squatted down so that her face was only inches from the wound. "Nah, you don't need stitches," she said in a conversation with herself. "It looks worse than it is." She cleaned Willow's skin and applied a bandage. "Which piece is yours?"

"Excuse me?"

"Your work pass. You're one of the artists, right?"

A normie spy.

"The horse," Willow said. "Thank you so much." She left before the woman had a chance to respond. An hour later, she was on the road to Reno, and a couple hours after that, she was back home in her dorm, watching blood circle around the shower drain until the water finally ran clear.

⁂

Ten years later, Willow returned to Burning Man after money problems had put her marriage in a vice grip. This time, she was prepared. She wasn't going to be a weekend warrior who showed up in time for some pictures and the Man and Temple burn and then left. Willow was part of the event this year, having brought her own piece, or more accurately, having found a more seasoned artist to help build and install her piece for her.

She brought her sister with her. Juniper was seven years younger; not many of their childhood years had overlapped. The last time Willow visited her parents, she saw that most of the pictures of her had been overtaken by ones of Juniper. Even the family dog, Chips, claimed more territory on the fireplace mantle. Evidence of Willow's recent divorce took the form of conspicuous gaps in the family picture displays. Rectangles of dust-free wood marked the places where her and her ex's wedding portraits recently stood. On the wall, Juniper's acceptance letter to UNLV law school had been framed and was positioned next to Willow's "Nevada Women in Business" certificate that looked to be printed from a template. It was offered as proof of Willow's work rather than marking an achievement. She framed it herself after beginning her multilevel marketing business, Natural Beauty. They hung it up before she'd started bleeding cash.

"It's not as hot as I thought it'd be," Juniper said. Willow handed her a tube of Natural Beauty sunblock. "Does this stuff actually work?"

"Of course it works. See for yourself." Willow had recently paid to put professional decals on her car advertising for Natural Beauty Consultants, and though she was proud of the work she'd done, how she'd put in a decade of cold calls and product parties to get to the top, she was embarrassed by the decal. The silhouette of a woman's face in profile was surrounded by bright pink hibiscus flowers, set above Willow's new slogan of "be true to you." Juniper opened the tube and squeezed it enough to get a waft of the scent.

"Smells like a Creamsicle."

"That's the orange extract. Tons of vitamin C." Willow pointed to the tiny-fonted list of ingredients, and Juniper shrugged as she took off her T-shirt to reveal a sports bra.

"Can you do my back?" Juniper asked. Willow generously applied the sunblock. She could feel the ridges of Juniper's rib-cage as she rubbed it into her skin. What she'd do to get her old metabolism back.

"What are you thinking for lunch?" Willow asked.

"I'm going to do the cleanse with you so that I can slim down a little before the semester starts. Let's have one of those juices after going out to explore? I want to see your sculpture!"

A pickup truck pulled up in the spot next to theirs. Two men hopped out and introduced themselves.

"Hey there, neighbors," one of them said. He looked like a bumble bee, flighty but with the hard-set jaw of someone whose words could sting. They looked like brothers, and Willow had a brief fantasy about her and Juniper each pairing off with one of them. But this was not a trip for flirting or rebounding. It was a trip to celebrate Willow's newfound path as an artistic creator and appreciator and Juniper's final acquiescence to her sister's request to be a face and body for the brand, at least for the summer before going off to law school. Willow came to the Black Rock Desert as one person, and she planned to leave as another. "That's quite the setup." The man waved his hand at the RV, generator, patio furniture, misters, and rug.

"Home sweet home," Willow said. "First time?"

"Eighth for me, sixth for him." The two men began setting up their camp wordlessly.

"Second for me, first for her. And she just turned twenty-two." Willow pointed an elbow toward her sister, whose cheeks were reddening.

"I'm jealous. You can't ever quite re-create the first time. Have a safe burn, you two. And happy belated birthday."

Willow poured herself a cup of her Invigorate teatox and filled both of their water bottles.

"Can I have some of the tea?"

"I brought those low-cal spiked lemonades you like. Do you want one of those instead? And I brought lots of food." Willow's hope that Juniper had forgotten about joining her in the detox dissipated. But maybe it would be a fun bonding experience. Maybe it would give them both a story to tell at parties, the kind of story where they took different parts in the retelling as if running lines for a play.

Willow had funded the art project herself. The phone booth was easy enough to find. She'd gotten it from an antique dealer in nearby Fernley. The shop was filled with the same kinds of items as in every antique store with "treasure" in the name: World War II memorabilia and portraits of muscle-bound Native Americans crafted by a white person in a fetishy fervor easily mistaken for artistic passion.

She and Juniper made the sign together. They worked slowly to carefully paint within the bubble letters' outlines. Willow wanted to be able to check in on her sister, and she could tell that her sister wanted to check in on her, too. Sometimes, it felt like each of them was the other's big sister.

As Willow rode her bike behind Juniper, she watched the wind blow her dyed red waves from side to side. They didn't look anything alike, and though she'd disliked the milkman jokes when they were younger, she certainly understood them. Their father, a horticulturalist, had championed the idea of naming them after plants. In adulthood, Willow worried that her worsening posture was slowly turning her into a weeping willow. And, like her namesake, Juniper was thriving, taking up space where she shouldn't be, certain that she would never leave after her strong roots reached down into the soil.

Their bikes' wheels, already coated in dust, whined and squeaked, marking the steadiness of their pedaling. Willow pedaled faster to catch up with Juniper.

"You don't even know where you're going," Willow said.

"I thought I'd be able to see it. But this is way bigger than I thought." Juniper braked hard enough to nearly toss her from the bike saddle. "Look at that!" She pointed at an art car meant to look like a ship. People were chanting "walk the plank" as a young guy in a onesie walked across the board to jump into another tall art car. A cross-armed Ranger surveyed the scene from beneath.

"Oh yeah. My first year, I spent more of the time on art cars.

It's a great way to see everything." Willow started pedaling again. She didn't wait to see if the guy made it to the other side.

Willow didn't want kids of her own, but when she looked back to see her sister still standing in awe of the art cars, she understood the impulse to see the world through younger, more hopeful eyes.

"Come on. It's really, really far out there."

⁂

The piece came together even better than she planned: a phone booth to Aphrodite. Juniper ditched her bike and ran inside the booth.

"It looks so good!"

They both went inside and picked up the phone's reccíver, positioning it in between their ears.

"You are beautiful and live this life so full. You are worth it. Be true to you," Juniper's ethereal voice spoke to them from the receiver. She'd been directed to "sound like a goddess" and had taken that direction excellently.

They hung it up and lifted it again to hear, "You contain multitudes and many admire your attitude. Like a raw diamond, you are natural perfection. Be true to you." Over and over, they listened to the five sets of affirmations. Juniper and Willow's combined script on the sign, covered in decorative foil, caught and catapulted the sun's light. Juniper had recommended they include relevant hashtags to promote Natural Beauty. They were small, tastefully tucked away in the lower right corner of the sign. Though she hadn't installed the piece herself, while she surveyed it, she felt a tenderness in her right palm, as if it'd been rubbed raw by a hammer's grip.

No one else was out here, and Willow started to feel faint, but the good kind of faint that teeters over the edge of euphoria. Her self-discipline had gotten her here.

"Make sure you're staying hydrated. By the time you feel thirsty, it's too late. You're already dehydrated." They both drank deeply, but Willow wasn't drinking water. She was finishing out the rest of her teatox. She wanted to take some pictures that night and didn't want to feel bloated. Each outfit had been carefully planned, and tonight's included a piece of lingerie that she'd sewn EL wire onto.

They posed for an elaborate series of pictures in front of the booth, and Willow took a couple of candid ones of her sister, her twisting her hair into a bun and one from behind as she surveyed their work, hands on hips. Willow said they should return to camp, but Juniper begged to go out to take pictures of the other art.

"The pictures will never do it justice," Willow warned.

"I know, but I want to at least try."

On their way to the dance tents that evening, it was too cold to wear the lingerie number. She pulled on her fur coat and offered her extra one to Juniper. Juniper hardly brought anything but herself and a complete openness to the new experiences she'd have. She was light and unencumbered, unlike Willow, who was weighted down by her past, present, and future—all heavy on her shoulders like buckets on a milkmaid's yoke. As the two walked, they kept with the flow of traffic on the Esplanade. Willow kept her jacket open, her hands in her pockets to widen the gap that showed the lace underneath. Though she knew this was not the kind of place where women were catcalled, she still mourned its absence. Juniper didn't say a word on their walk.

"I have something you should see, something I found when I was riding around today," Juniper said. She reached for Willow's hand and helped her weave through burners who, in the darkness, had begun to morph into different versions of the same person. "They ripped you off."

Across from a kinky circus theme camp and kitty corner from a gladiator ring stood an unmarked phone booth. A few people wandered in and out of the booth. They all came out smiling.

"What is that?" Willow asked a man exiting. He wore a blazer and neon running shorts and looked younger from behind than he did when he turned to face her.

"The Talk to God booth." He smiled a helpful person's smile. Willow felt like it was getting darker still, like walking into a room with the lights off when your eyes refuse to refocus. He seemed to be fading in and out.

"That's my sister's idea. We worked on it for hours. They stole it!"

"They bring this piece out every year. I think they've been doing it for ten or fifteen, at least." He shrugged. Juniper looked from the man to Willow and back to the man again. Willow's body told her to sit down, and she listened. When she tried to stand up, it demanded that she lay down instead. Willow needed to leave. As soon as her body would let her, she'd be hauling that RV back to Reno. While people watched the Man burn, she and her sister would be in their pajamas, slimy sheet masks made to look like cartoon animals on their faces.

"Is she okay?" he asked. His concern seemed genuine even though he was already turning his body away from them in the direction of a departure.

"It's just fucked up," Juniper barked.

"I'm sorry," Willow said. "I didn't know."

"We'll get our booth closer to the action next year." Juniper rubbed her sister's back in wide circles. Thumps of bass shook the Earth beneath them, and Willow felt the rumbling as if it were inside of her, the aftershocks of an earthquake that everybody saw coming.

⁂

The night before her forty-eighth birthday, Willow was in a car accident, T-boned by someone on their phone. The injuries looked bad, but the prognosis was good.

"You're so lucky," the ER's attending physician said. "If the paramedics got there any later, you would be in much worse shape. It'll be hard work, but I'm confident that you'll fully recover." Willow guessed that the doctor said this to everyone who was staring down the barrel of a months-long recovery. Hope can heal. She'd heard that from a therapist on a talk show once.

After months of rehab, juggling appointments with specialists (who then referred her to other specialists) with her daytime job in HR at Solartech Energy Company, Willow began to lose faith that hope would heal her fully. She still got shooting pains in her left leg. It felt like the muscles in her back were always tightening around her spinal column like a python. Headaches were a part of her everyday life, and her boss at Solartech never believed her when she said that she couldn't come in because of them. But people with kids regularly left in the middle of the day or took the entire day off for their "sick kiddos." She was much older than her colleagues and had trouble managing the constant software updates. They hadn't covered any of that in her online HR professional training.

Since the accident, she had gained nearly sixty pounds, which worsened her joint pain. She hadn't changed her diet or what her doctors referred to as her "health habits" or "lifestyle choices" since before, but the weight kept on coming. Though she resented the dull ache in her lower back and knees, she was struck by the idea that there was now more of her than ever. There was philosophical power to that.

In the waiting rooms of chiropractors, physiotherapists, acupuncturists, and massage therapists, Willow ran out of reading material. Scrolling through her phone made her think about the kid that T-boned her, though she never actually got proof that they were on their phone.

While waiting for her 2:00 appointment at Northern Nevada Chiropractic Care one day, Willow pulled out the letter she'd picked up at her mailbox that morning. It was from her sister, and she sometimes carried around letters from her sister for weeks before opening them. They were like a fire extinguisher she knew would be there when she needed it. Break glass in the case of an emergency.

The clock on the waiting room wall kept ticking without the second hand moving forward. Time passed, but its marker stayed put, which felt eerie. There was no calming music. The doctor was already running an hour late, and her boss would have a lecture about teamwork ready for her when she returned. This was an emergency.

Willow delicately unsealed the envelope. Seeing the familiar curve of Juniper's child-like handwriting, a print/cursive hybrid, made the imagined lecture from her boss vanish. No matter how far apart they lived, Willow took comfort in knowing how her sister's capital Ls would tilt, how the big bubble of her Ps would loom over other letters. When she unfolded the letter, a beautifully designed piece of rectangular cardstock fell from the folds. She recognized the stick figure man immediately. Juniper's letter did not contain the usual updates about the kids and their mother's new embroidery business. It said only, "You deserve this. xoxo." The pages were back issues of the official Burning Man newsletter, *The Jack Rabbit Speaks*. She learned about the biggest art projects, strategies on reducing the event's carbon footprint, administrative updates regarding the Bureau of Land Management. The newsletter was funny, written by someone who was allowed to use their sharp tongue. She imagined herself back out on the playa, no appointments, no unannounced performance reviews, no medication adjustments, no software updates. Just her talking to a lady drinking from a cup strapped to her neck.

It was impossible to get a ticket these days. In the name of fairness, the organization had moved to a lottery system, and though she'd put in for a ticket a few times over the years, she'd never successfully secured one. She tilted the ticket so that the overhead fluorescent light revealed the holographic image of the Man. When her name was finally called by the receptionist, Willow allowed herself one more moment to admire her golden ticket.

This year, Willow planned to stay for three nights. She could only take one day off of work, so although she would've liked to stay for longer, she chose to see the bright side of only being out in the desert for a few days. *Hope can heal.*

The event was not easy to get around. Her knees ached, and when she tried to ride her bike, it sunk into the playa mud. She decided to stay on foot instead. Willow prioritized comfort over costume, though she enjoyed seeing how creative people were, reveling in the generosity of their imaginative spirits. At one point, she passed the Talk to God phone booth, and she tried to forget her own art project years and years ago. When she conjured the memory of her and Juniper taking photos in front of their creation, it was too blurry to make out the specifics, which was fine with her because she didn't want the specifics to come into focus. It was better that the person she was then lived in pictures and other artifacts. Artifacts can be buried.

She left her uncharged phone in her car while she explored. If she wanted to remember something, she slowly closed her eyes to take a mental picture, a strategy that a therapist had once recommended to her. By Saturday, she was slow-blinking so frequently that it felt like she was watching a stop motion film. She took in snippets of a roller rink, a statue of a woman at least thirty feet tall, a couple having a wedding ceremony at dusk, two toddlers doing handstands in Kidsville, an acrobat suspended above her by a silk rope, a masked improv troupe at Center Camp.

She was too tired to watch the Man burn on Saturday night, so she fell asleep to the distant bass that reverberated off of her camper's walls, a heartbeat that made her feel like she was inside a metallic womb.

The next day was the same. She packed in as much as she could, gifting people with earnest compliments and a listening ear. In front of her camp on D Street, this year called Dearly Beloved, she set up a table marked only by a sheet of printer paper that read "Complaints for Compliments." Few people wandered by on their bikes on their way to and from the Esplanade, and she tried to make those few interactions count. One couple took a seat in the two metal folding chairs positioned in front of Willow's table. They complained about how they weren't able to value each other in the Default World like they were at Burning Man. Willow nodded as they aired their grievances to the point of exhaustion. Big complaints collided with small complaints until they all seemed to lose their meaning. *Your mother has never accepted me. You cook meat even though the smell makes me sick. You don't respect my love language. You don't acknowledge my emotional labor. You load the dishwasher wrong.*

They seemed to figure it all out. They needed to make more compromises. "See. I knew your love would get you through this. You are a beautiful couple," she said. "Have a wonderful burn."

On Sunday, Willow planned to attend the Temple burn. Unlike the Man burn, the Temple burn was somber, a lament to the Man burn's high energy DJ set. She wandered through the structure, which was delicately pieced together using the thinnest pieces of wood she'd ever seen. It looked like a house of cards. Pluck out one of these pieces, and the entire structure would come tumbling down. The Temple's walls served as a place for public grieving. Willow calculated the length of people's lives. A man named Greg had lived to the age of 42; a woman named Eloise had lived to 96. A cat named Bradford had lived to 14. A child named Mary had lived eight days. Inside, Burning Man's sounds were muffled. Some people cried. Other people whispered. Strangers hugged and held hands; grief's centripetal force brought everyone's bodies closer together. Willow found herself crying in an older man's embrace. They exchanged no words as they swayed back and forth.

Willow fished a picture she'd brought of herself posing in front of the wild horse sculpture out of the front pocket of her shirt. She pinned it to the wall so that it was part of the mosaic of faces. Hers was the only face frowning.

Hours later, the Temple burned, and Willow tried to follow the path of different flames. She imagined the photo of herself blackening and then curling at the corners. The smell of burning wood encircled her. Two spires on the structure simultaneously ignited. Soon, the fire would be put out, the crowds would leave, and Willow would be left to watch the ashes swirl around, scattering her memories across the Black Rock Desert.

5

ALTERNATE ROUTE SUGGESTED

KENNY WAS TWENTY-ONE WHEN HIS son was born. Now, at twenty-two, he regularly revised the last several months, cnvisioning himself as an author of the choose-your-own-adventure books he'd read when he was younger. He'd always read all the possible endings before choosing the best path and wished that someone had done the same for his actual life.

In different ways, each of the men in his life had done just that—one uncle became a computer programmer and moved to the Bay Area, while another uncle dealt blackjack at the Gold Dust West in Reno. Before he left Kenny and his mom, his dad had fallen somewhere in the middle, with an associate's in science and a job as a petroleum technician. None of these paths looked like one he'd want to follow, though.

For now, he worked as a retail security guard at Clothing Outpost, an occupational placeholder for something better. Upholding the single responsibility of preventing people from stealing merchandise had worn tracks of monotony in his mind that could only be rerouted by his strongest, most vivid daydreams.

On a December day sharpened by the teeth of biting cold, Kenny had been at his post by the entrance/exit for an hour before a woman about his age triggered the alarm, bringing a flush to her cheeks.

She was prettier than most of the girls who shopped there. Her wavy hair hung all the way down near her waist. Kenny couldn't make himself report her theft. *[See alternate route 1 if you would like Kenny to report the shoplifter.]* He'd watched her walk into a dressing room with an armful of summer dresses and underwear and walk out with only a pair of denim shorts, likely her own, hastily hung crooked on their hanger. Her backpack, which he hadn't seen when she walked into the dressing room, was now full. She was smart and had bought a tin of mints, so that if one of the security tags set off the alarm, she could pull the supposed culprit out of the flimsy plastic bag. Kenny gave an almost imperceptible nod as she hurried through the doors. If she came back, she might remember his generosity. And if his supervisor, Ron, reviewed the tapes (which he frequently threatened, but never did), he planned to say that her backpack was smaller than the ones depicted on the NO LARGE BAGS ALLOWED sign bolted to the building's stucco façade.

On his lunch break, Kenny walked three doors down to Pizza Plus and ordered two slices and a Coke. He chewed on the left side; one of his back right molars had been bothering him. An apparently unattended kid slammed his fists onto the pinball machine

Alternate Route 1. After weighing the options, though, he decided it best to report her. He asked to see inside of her backpack, and she offered it too eagerly, as if her innocence were stored in a secret zippered pocket. He dug through her bag, which smelled like too-ripe strawberries, but none of the clothes had tags on them. "Those are mine," she said. "They're not from here." Without any tags to prove otherwise, he sent her on her way, muttering an apology.

to dislodge the ball. The cashier didn't stop him, so Kenny didn't either. If that were his kid, he'd intervene and tilt the machine from side to side. But it wasn't. Kenneth Jr. was at home with Kenny's ex-girlfriend Jade, and she was packing up their things as he ate his slice. By the time he finished his shift, they'd be halfway to Sacramento.

He foresaw what might become an ugly custody battle with Jade and pictured himself wearing a tailored suit—something much nicer than the off-brand separates sold at Clothing Outpost—as he presented his case to the family court judge. As soon as he got back into classes, he'd graduate and go to law school, then move to the East Coast. Become a partner and get enough money to move KJ out there with him. *[See alternate route 2 if you think Kenny should go to law school.]* Maybe even make amends with Jade, promise to never cheat again, and bring her out there too.

Alternate Route 2. What once seemed like an abstract aspiration took on a concrete shape three years later, when Kenny took the LSAT and scored in the top 2 percent of test-takers. He didn't even have to apply to schools; recruiters were coming after him, leaving cheerfully aggressive voicemails on his phone. His mom celebrated by buying an oversized cookie from Mrs. Fields at the mall; an employee had written *One Smart Cookie* on the top in neon green frosting. But he didn't feel like a smart cookie once he started taking classes. The panic attacks happened during finals the first semester, the nervous breakdown during the second semester, and the withdrawal from the university during the summer that followed. When later asked why he'd dropped out, he answered that attorneys were assholes.

After refilling his soda, he drank it down partway to refill it once more, then pulled two quarters from his pocket and laid them on the pinball's glass top for the boy to use. He took his time on the walk back to work, careful to use every minute of his break. On the floor, he wasn't allowed to check his phone, but he felt it vibrate six times before the second half of his shift was over. Once he was able to check it, he didn't; he already knew what the texts said. At least one from his mom saying he needed to visit his Uncle Jeff, the card dealer, in hospice care, and then the other five from Jade saying that she'd left and would need him to start sending her money, a picture of KJ thrown in as an exclamation point on the end of the demand.

But he was off about the ratio. Five texts from his mom were about Uncle Jeff, and only one from Jade that said, *Pass is closed. Waiting til 2morrow.* He drove straight to Sierra Nevada Hospice and Palliative Care Center.

The woman at the front desk voiced a greeting without looking at him, which made the weighty guilt he felt for not visiting sooner slide off his shoulders. He'd always liked his uncle; it wasn't that. He just couldn't bring himself to be in a place like this—or, more accurately, the place he'd imagined whenever his mom told him she'd visited.

The care center was nicer than the place in his imagination. A color palette of pale neutrals, accented by maroon, covered the walls and furniture. Maybe he would consider going into design. From the days when he'd used a level to hang a Metallica poster (he'd even framed it) to when he'd assembled KJ's nursery furniture from Target, he'd always had a knack for interior design. *[See alternate route 3 if you think Kenny should pursue a career in interior design.]*

"Could you tell me where room 203 is?" he asked the woman. She pulled out a map and showed him where the room was before

Alternate Route 3. Kenny promised himself that when he got home, he would start to research how to become an interior designer. He kept the promise, but not for long. He learned that having good taste and an eye for design were tiny slivers of an enormous pie. Even if he took some classes, there wouldn't be any entry level jobs available in town, and moving somewhere with a higher cost of living was out of the question. He still put together a modest portfolio, composed of pictures of his apartment, and stashed it inside a manila folder at the bottom of what Jade called the junk drawer.

offering to give it to him. He refused and walked down the hallway and up the stairs. Once he got to the second floor, he wished he'd taken the map— the floor was a labyrinth of visiting and recreation areas, all vacant. They seemed like the kinds of spaces that would look good on a glossy brochure.

He knocked gently as he opened the door. His mom's face looked red-raw and tear-streamed as she bent over her brother. His uncle's eyelids were closed, but Kenny could see the soft vibrations that he hoped meant he was dreaming. A quiet beeping sound tracked the strained work of his uncle's failing heart. The tubes and machines unsettled Kenny, but his mom deftly maneuvered around them. Years of work as a nurse aide guided her fingers around hospital gown hems and IV catheters.

"Kenny's here to see you, Jeff." She rubbed his hand, but he did not respond.

"Hi, Uncle Jeff," Kenny offered in a hoarse voice. His uncle didn't move, not even when a nurse came in to fuss with the machines and replace bags of clear liquid. She smelled like cinnamon, and had lips so shiny with gloss that Kenny couldn't help imagining what it might feel like to softly press his own lips against them. He looked out the window opposite her, worried that making eye contact with her would reveal the contents of his reverie. This was the kind of out-of-his-league girl his friends would goad him into flirting with, the kind of girl he did flirt with if he'd had enough to drink.

After the nurse left, Kenny's mom asked about Jade and KJ in mumbles, and Kenny mumbled responses in kind. This was a part of their communication routine, one that appeared fuller and more satisfying than it actually was, the loaf of white bread crushed at the bottom of a heavy grocery bag.

"They're saying this could be his last day," his mom said. "And that they want to make him as comfortable as possible. But we don't believe that, do we?" She shook her head, as if absorbing, then transmitting, Jeff's response.

"He'll be okay," Kenny said. He crossed his arms, then shoved his hands deep into his pockets. "I don't mean he'll be okay, but it will all be okay."

"I wish you were right," she said and laced her fingers back through Jeff's.

"I'm so sorry, but I have to go. That's Jade, and she's leaving tonight." He gestured to his cell phone, though he had not received any messages. "And sorry I didn't come sooner."

His mom closed her eyes and gave a solemn nod, disapproval in slow motion. He waved at his uncle, feeling deep in his gut, the place where he stored every devastating truth, that this was likely the last time he'd see him. He hated goodbyes, and not because they seemed too final, but because people always *wanted* them to feel final.

Once he got outside, he breathed in the cold until it felt like sharp crystals had bloomed inside his chest. With that breath came a dull throb in his tooth that he chose to disregard. He thought of his mom standing there alone, the other family members still making their way by car and airplane, and considered going back inside. But he realized that he'd already begun driving away.

⁂

Jade drew back the deadbolt halfway through him unlocking the door, which meant she was in a generous mood. KJ was crying, a fact she announced in between his wails. Kenny picked him up, ran through the potential reasons for crying, and stopped after smelling his diaper. He handed him a toy shaped as a bumblebee affixed to a quilt, which made the sound of crinkling paper when handled. The crying stopped as KJ wrapped his mouth around an antenna, and Kenny picked him up to show Jade how quickly he'd fixed the problem. But she was already silently cooking dinner, breaking spaghetti noodles in half to fit in the small pot and exploding pasta shards across the kitchen counter in the process. He turned on the TV, then brought the toy to KJ's face in big loopy movements, doing his best to mimic the sound of an airplane's propeller.

"So, the pass is still closed?" he asked over the sound of a newscaster describing the suspect in a hit-and-run accident.

"That's what I texted you."

Kenny didn't have a good response, so he triangulated KJ into the conversation.

"You don't want to go yet anyway, huh?" He kissed the back of KJ's head, which seemed to startle him.

"Let's not do this again. I'm tired." Kenny knew he didn't have the patience, energy, or desire to be with KJ all day, but that didn't quiet the voice in his head that wanted to ask, *Tired from doing what exactly?*

He nodded before putting KJ in his bouncer and taking over dinner duty by straining the pasta, which was now overcooked. A car alarm sounded in the parking lot in time with a sharp pain that flashed in Kenny's molar. He'd get it fixed as soon as he was able to become full time and could get insurance. Ron had said he could bump up his hours as soon as Lisa went down to part time after her foot surgery. Kenny had found himself staring at Lisa's foot the last few days, imagining the footbones flexing and then retreating beneath her pale, mottled skin. She'd caught him once and asked what he was staring at, and in a panic, he complimented her pink platform flip-flops. *[See alternate route 4 if you think Kenny should contact Lisa.]*

Sitting at the kitchen table, Kenny tongued the top of his molar as if to scoop out the pain. Jade silently handed KJ over. Normally, he cried during the handoff, but this time he didn't. Still, he made a soft whimper that made Kenny feel like his tooth was set to vibrate. He and Jade ate in silence, and Jade got ready for bed without reciprocating Kenny's call of goodnight.

KJ fell asleep on Kenny's chest as he clicked through TV channels, a part of his nightly meditative ritual. Click, a baseball game. Click, a woman mincing a clove of garlic. Click, a man in black and

Alternate Route 4. Kenny Facebook-messaged Lisa, halfway hoping that Jade would ask who he was talking to in an eager voice pitched high by jealousy. He asked how Lisa was feeling and whether or not she was still getting the surgery. No response. In another message, he explained that if she was worried about someone covering for her, she didn't need to. Kenny could cover all of her shifts. No response. He said her foot was starting to look bad. No response. He sent the first image of a gnarled foot yielded by a Google search. No response. He apologized. Two hours later, she blocked him.

white struggling to connect a sprayer to a hose as a booming voice exclaimed, "Only three payments of $19.95."

The next morning, Kenny saw that he'd missed twelve phone calls. Uncle Jeff had died; his mom had not left a voicemail, but that was what twelve calls meant. Jade had already left for the day, and he vaguely recalled something she'd said about a doctor's appointment for KJ. He grimaced at the memory of the last well-visit when the doctor had said that KJ was only in the fiftieth percentile for height, and the fortieth percentile for weight. Thankfully, the doctor had looked at Jade while delivering the news, an accusation reserved for her alone.

He drafted a text asking where she'd gone, then deleted it. His shift started in a half hour, and he waited to call his mom until five minutes before he had to clock in. She delivered the news without crying; he was probably the eighth or ninth person she'd had to say the same thing to. *I'm sorry*, he said in his head, but aloud, he said, "Thank you. Thank you for telling me."

⁂

The next day, the tooth pain had gotten so severe that he'd stopped eating solid foods altogether. Lisa ended up quitting, but that didn't equate to a promotion to full time. Ron explained that he'd made a mistake in promising more hours. The security staff had a different designation than other employees. They were independent contractors, and consequently could never be salaried employees with 401(k)s and insurance member IDs and paid vacation time. Kenny now felt an empty camaraderie with the gray-haired man who patrolled the whole strip mall.

Kenny spent his entire lunch break in a bathroom stall trying to get a picture of his tooth using different angles, flash and no flash, zoom and no zoom. The tooth looked normal, a bodily betrayal. It made him feel like when his car made clunking sounds on the way to the mechanic but stopped the moment someone wearing coveralls turned the key in the ignition.

He counted the customers coming into and leaving the store to keep his mind active, his shifts punctuated by the automatic glass doors' squeal. An older man walking with the aid of crutches was the fifteenth person to exit this shift. Customer number fifteen set off the alarm and said, "Are you fucking kidding me" as he tried to balance one crutch against his body and search for his receipt.

Kenny began looking through the bag before Ron ran up in between them.

"My apologies, sir. He's new." Kenny considered correcting him to say he'd been there for a year, but before he could, Ron added, "Thank you for your service." Kenny hadn't noticed the hat, which had *Vietnam Veteran* embroidered in gold thread above the bill. He also hadn't noticed that his hand was still inside the bag in between a faux leather belt and a black dress shirt.

"Yes, thank you," Kenny said as he pulled his hand from the bag. At the end of his shift, he considered hanging up the blue vest that constituted his uniform for the last time, maybe leaving a note explaining why he'd quit, but his tooth ached in warning. *[See alternate route 5 if you think Kenny should quit.]*

After work, his phone vibrated, alerting him that it would be his and Jade's four-year anniversary, if they were still together. Another snowstorm had kept Jade in Sparks, and they'd reached a place of peaceful coexistence that Kenny sometimes confused for contentedness.

On the way home, he stopped at the grocery store to buy her flowers. These kinds of gestures always worked with her. Their senior year of high school, she'd rejected him the first three times he

Alternate Route 5. Fuck it, he thought. I can do better than this place, this job. I deserve the same respect as a vet on crutches. He flipped Ron off and yelled "I quit!" But Ron didn't seem to hear or see him. He'd moved back to the register to show one of the new guys how to process a return. Kenny repeated himself, and he got Ron's attention that time. Ron shrugged as a parent might when a child refuses to eat his vegetables. Disappointed, but not surprised—resigned to the reality that people often don't do what's best for them. Kenny caught his own reflection in the full-length mirror on the end of the blazer rack, his right arm and middle finger still extended in the air, and smiled. On the drive home, adrenaline quickened his pulse and made him clamp down his jaw. Fuck that place, he growled from behind gritted teeth. His molar throbbed, but he couldn't make his face go lax. He needed to get to a bar with some friends, tell them over tequila shots how he'd gone out with a bang. The accelerator depressed until it couldn't go any farther, his sedan pushed to its v4 engine's limits. He was going too fast and the roads were too slick, a realization that came too late, seconds after his car spun around into oncoming traffic.

asked her out, but the fourth time worked. He'd gone all out for his promposal, arranging a scavenger hunt that spanned the entire city and even made it onto the community page of the *Sparks Tribune*.

In the parking lot, he looked up the meaning of different flowers on his phone, and he thought of the first time he saw Uncle Jeff's faded tattoo of a thorny rose on his shoulder at the Minden Community Pool. He'd inspected it for a full minute before Jeff volunteered an explanation that the tattoo was in honor of his ex-wife, the thorniest bitch he'd ever known.

In the grocery store, Kenny frowned at the condensation in the flowers' glass case. These flowers, even the most vibrantly colored ones, were in the process of dying. An employee with perfectly curled, stiff ringlets watered the potted plants next to the case and joked that Kenny must be in the doghouse. Hastened by embarrassment, he grabbed the purple carnations that had been sprinkled with glitter. Only once he got back to his car did he remember that purple carnations symbolized unpredictability.

He stopped at a drive-thru to get a side of mashed potatoes and ate in his car in the apartment's parking lot. Since KJ was born, Kenny and Jade had begun a silent fight to prove who was the most adult, and eating fast food instead of making something at home felt too young, something a teenager who just got his first car would do. Currently, Jade was winning the fight. She figured out how to put the utilities in her name when they moved into the apartment together. She alerted the waitstaff when they got Kenny's order wrong. Kenny's molar felt as if it'd split in half, and nausea enveloped him as he balled up the paper bag his food had come in and slammed it into the garbage can.

The apartment was empty, a note reading "Left for Sac—will be back next week for everything else" lay on the couch, the placement a final insult sourced from his nightly TV-watching ritual. Kenny arranged the flowers in a tall glass and staged them for a picture to send to Jade. He wrote a text that said, *Happy anniversary :(*, and sent the picture. There was no reason to believe that Jade wasn't going to leave, and yet he still felt shocked as he stood in the half-empty apartment. He'd imagined how he'd smoothed things over so many times that he'd forgotten that he'd been the one to cause any ripples in the first place.

He heard a desperate knock at the door, and he rushed to open it. When he swung the door open, he only saw his neighbor Ben, completely at ease.

"What is it?" Kenny asked.

"I saw Jade moving her stuff out. Kind of fucked up that you didn't help her."

"I guess so," Kenny said. His neighbor forced his way inside in a way that didn't feel like he was forcing his way inside.

"Rent's going up. Did you see the notice?" Kenny hadn't seen the notice but nodded anyway. "Can I see the layout? It trips me out to see all of my apartment, but backward." Kenny nodded again, and Ben walked away to begin his self-guided tour. Kenny knew what was coming next. Ben was going to ask to move in. He'd made a joke about it once before when they were doing laundry, likely prompted by hearing one of Kenny and Jade's fights through the wall. "Everything split right down the middle," he'd offered, and now that Jade was gone, so was her dad's offer to pay rent for the first year they were in the apartment.

"In my apartment, the second bedroom and the bathroom are right across from each other." He pointed his arms in opposite directions as if directing airplane passengers to the emergency exits. *[See alternate route 6 if you think Kenny should move in with Ben.]*

"What's up?" Ben asked.

"What?"

"Are you okay?" Ben moved in closer, squinting his eyes.

"Your cheek's all fucked up." Kenny touched his cheek to survey his facial topography, a small mountain now rising from above his jaw. His face was hot to the touch, and the mashed potatoes threatened to rise up from his stomach.

"It's just a bad tooth," he reassured Ben, who'd taken up his elbow.

Alternate Route 6. The longer Ben stood in front of Kenny, the more the prospect of them moving in together made sense. He'd never had the college roommate experience and imagined what it might be like. Would they grocery shop together like he did with Jade? Would they develop inside jokes and watch the same shows? Would the middle of their shared interest Venn diagram expand until their circles overlapped completely? No, no, and no, as it turned out. Ben didn't allow KJ to visit, said having a baby in the apartment ruined his vibe. Ben spent most of his time watching YouTube videos that explained which politicians were lizard people and how 9/11 was an inside job. Kenny only lasted four months before he broke the lease and moved in with his mom, camping out on a rollaway in the living room.

"I think you need to go to the hospital. It looks really bad."

"No insurance."

"Just go to the emergency room. They have to take everyone."

Kenny refused Ben's offer to take him. As he drove, he imagined being an EMT, watching the cars pull off to the side of the road in deference to the ambulance's siren. Maybe he could enroll in the EMT program at Western Nevada College. *[See alternate route 7 if you think Kenny should become an EMT.]*

Once he got to the hospital, he parked and walked slowly. Each careful step was an attempt to keep his tooth unbothered by movement. The emergency room doors squealed in the same pitch as the ones at work, which reminded him to send a text message to Ron saying that he wouldn't be able to come in the next day. He felt the

Alternate Route 7. Years later, when Kenny came to talk to KJ's second grade class, he described this day as the day he decided to leave his dead-end job to start helping people. The kids in KJ's class were impressed by the defibrillator he'd brought and hadn't seemed interested in the story about his uncle. So, instead, he recounted the time that he'd brought a man who'd been pronounced dead back to life. KJ's teacher cut him off mid-story, which was good because he'd already begun to embellish. At KJ's high school graduation, KJ embellished Kenny's story further during his valedictorian speech. He urged his classmates to show the same bravery his father had throughout his life, which was cut short when he helped save eight people after the bombing at the federal building in Carson City. KJ would never learn that his father hadn't actually died saving anyone; he'd died under concrete, having hesitated too long at the building's crumbling entrance. KJ closed his speech by saying that they all could be heroes, and each of their hero's journeys had already begun.

weight of the phrase "emergency room" as he typed it, and before checking in with the woman sitting at the front desk, he updated his status on Facebook to *Having the worst Monday ever. At the* ER.

Jade liked the post, so he deleted it. He called his mom, but hung up before she could answer. She had enough worries of her own, and he didn't want to add this to the list. Though now that he thought about it, he had never been to the doctor without her.

"It's my tooth," Kenny said as the woman seated at the desk handed him a form on a clipboard. She had a warm smile and tired eyes, looked a little like his mom. As he spoke, air rushed into his mouth and attacked the tooth. He didn't know some of the answers to the form's questions and had to guess the name of the medication he was allergic to. Some kind of antibiotic, he knew that much. He texted his mom to ask, adding "just wondering." Kenny was a bad liar, and when his mom asked where he was, he told her. Hot tears of relief and embarrassment streamed down his face. He wiped them away before submitting his paperwork.

Ron texted him that he could take the remainder of his permitted sick leave, but only if he could get one of the other security officers to cover his shift. Kenny didn't have any of their numbers, and didn't even know their full names. What if he wasn't able to get anyone to cover for him? How would he have enough money for KJ? How would he be able to pay his rent? Would he have to move into his mom's one-bedroom way out in Lemmon Valley?

The questions kept coming even as he shook them away. The list of hypotheticals moved from possible to probable at a dizzying pace. He could even feel the verb tenses shifting from conditional to future, from what he could do to what he was going to do. That sense of inevitability—of working in a casino and then meeting a new, less kind Jade, and then having another KJ by accident—nauseated him.

After several deep breaths, the feeling subsided, but pain returned to replace it. When he heard his name being called, he shook his head and hoped that if he continued to stare intently at the door, his mom would appear. She didn't appear, and he wondered if he'd even told her where he was. His memories were beginning to feel incomplete, and his sense of chronology had gotten scrambled.

A nurse in scrubs patterned with cats wearing stethoscopes took his temperature. He tried to follow the words coming out of her mouth but couldn't focus. Something about an abscess and an infection spreading. The question about allergies came up again, and he shook his head, more to communicate that he couldn't bear the pain of opening his mouth again than in answer to the question.

He awoke woozy with anesthesia and the faint feeling that he'd done something embarrassing. On the morning after his twenty-first birthday, he'd woken up with the same feeling and figured most things out as if assembling a puzzle with the foreknowledge that a few pieces would never be found. He'd said something to make Jade cry, a prediction about her never leaving Sparks, getting fat on the free Pizza Plus slices that'd be a perk of her job working there. *[See alternate route 8 if you think Kenny should contact Jade.]*

Then, he remembered thrashing around, the nurse trying to calm him down, the security personnel being called in when that didn't work. His mom was now in the room with him, and the dark circles under her eyes seemed more permanent than they had before. She held his hand as she'd held her brother's and shook her head in gentle reproach.

Alternate Route 8. After the dizziness subsided, he called Jade, and she answered before it even rang. He asked her to come see him and apologized for everything, begged her to come back. He would be better for her. She deserved better. KJ was laughing in the background, and Kenny asked if he could at least see KJ. She didn't respond, and the silence intensified his dizziness. He tried to focus on one spot on the wall to steady himself, settling on the pain scale chart. One to ten on the left, a range of smiling then frowning faces on the right. We'll come and see you soon, she said, and the thought of all three of them together became the force that steadied him.

"Why didn't you call me sooner?" she asked.

Kenny couldn't answer. Instead, he slid his tongue through the hole where his tooth had been, lingering on the slick emptiness before imagining what his smile might look like with a set of bright white veneers.

6

CONVENTIONS

AFTER ARRIVING AT HER HOTEL room, Melissa peeled off her shapewear, then kicked her heels across the room. The shoes landed with two light thuds next to the air conditioner, which growled in response. The smell of something chemical, freon maybe, traveled across the room. She pulled out her essential oils and diffuser, the culprits that necessitated she check a bag instead of carrying one on as her father always recommended. A few droplets of *Relax, Rejuvenate* camouflaged the offending smell. She rubbed her feet, which ached after two tight layovers had her running in shoes that weren't even intended for walking. She had a big enough online platform to be recognized in airports, and she prioritized style over comfort in pursuit of that recognition.

Digital wind chimes alerted her that she had two texts: one from her husband, Andrew, and one from her newest online suitor Mikael. She liked when their messages came in around the same time; it made her feel like the two men were occupying the same space, and she could easily toggle between them. She fantasized about inviting them both to a party, dividing her attention equally between them. One shoulder squeeze for Andrew, one kiss for Mikael. One compliment for Andrew, one drink refill for Mikael. Of course they would never meet in person; Melissa was careful. She kept her DMs open, but it took a lot for her to respond to someone, and the exchanges never extended beyond mild flirtation. For every response she sent, there were thirty other compliments-turned-solicitations-turned-insults-turned-threats that remained unopened.

Melissa delicately laid out neon-colored index cards in a five-by-two grid on the bed's comforter, then picked up each to rehearse the ten parts of her speech. Maybe this time she would change the introduction to something with a little more kick to it. She was in Texas, after all. She changed her opening line to, "Welcome to Ladies Empower Ladies! I'm here today to help you embrace your inner boss bitch! [Wait for applause]." To her knowledge, attendees had to be at least sixteen years old, so she decided the strong language should be fine, even capitalized the double Bs so she'd remember to emphasize them.

She opened Andrew's text. In it, he explained that he needed her last bank statement for their home loan preapproval ASAP. Perhaps, he suggested, they should actually combine their finances as they'd decided to six months before, when they'd gotten married. Melissa had thought she was pregnant, and even when it turned out to be a false alarm, she'd fallen for the thin sense of security and stability making plans provided and couldn't stop making them. A baby, a husband, a house.

When Melissa first met Andrew, she was broke. After dropping out of college, she had struggled to keep a full-time job; the reason for termination cited by her last boss was insubordination, and the boss before that cited threats against fellow employees. Of course, these were both codes for her aggressively rejecting their offers for after-work drinks.

She blamed her father for teaching her to always speak her mind, which carved out a perpetual guilt in her gut that sometimes made her feel sick. She imagined the negative energy of that blame barreling toward her father, shocking the cells in his lungs into unstoppable multiplication. An energy healer she'd seen assured her this was impossible, but Melissa's hypothesis made as much sense as the "real" cause of equally invisible radon gas. Every time she visited her father, parts of him were disappearing—his hair thinning, his broad shoulders narrowing—and she imagined each image as a page in a flip-book she was flipping through too quickly. The beauty tutorials Melissa had begun doing initially served as a needed distraction from her father's illness, but her technique and charisma soon earned her tens of thousands of views and several offers from beauty industry companies to create sponsored posts.

In her hotel, Melissa cozied under the comforter before opening Mikael's text. He'd sent her a short video of him flexing his pecs, sweat-slicked after a workout, to the beat of a heavy metal song she didn't know. She texted back and forth with Mikael, posing for pictures in the plush ivory robe she'd packed. She'd also brought a Lavish Selfie Mount—the product that, thanks to her branded content posts on Instagram, was now selling by the hundreds—for her own use. Not only could these mounts stick to any surface, they also featured a light at the bottom that was "more flattering and more natural than any filter."

After reviewing the pictures, she retrieved her notepad that had the word "Goaldigger" embossed in gold font. This is where she kept all of her lists: short- and long-term aspirations, new video concepts, and, hidden on the last page, a running list of her inadequacies. The number of items on this list never decreased, though it did change. "Disgusting double chin" became "Angular jaw looks too masculine" after she'd lost twenty pounds on the keto diet.

She snapped a few more pictures to post on the social media pages for her company, Babelicious, after using a Korean beauty app to soften the edges of her jaw and enlarge her eyes. Then, she texted Andrew that she would send the bank statements if there was a break in her packed convention schedule the next day.

⁂

Before walking out on stage, Melissa rearranged her body parts in her clothes so that everything looked smooth: pulled up her high-waisted skirt and tights, re-tucked in her silk blouse. Someone wearing a headset appeared and clipped a microphone onto Melissa's blazer lapel. She shuffled back through her notecards one last time before making her way to the podium. The enormous screen behind her showcased her full name in hot pink letters and the title of her talk, "Womentrepeneurs under 30 Work It." She couldn't make out any individual faces because of the stage lights, but she could hear distinct voices shout out two of her video sign-offs: "Get it done, girl!" and "Makeup is magic!"

The crowd went wild from her address to fellow boss bitches onward. She described her journey from dropping out of college to becoming an influencer who had companies lining up to get the coveted Babelicious endorsement. Success in her business doesn't come easy, she warned. The cute little five-minute makeup tutorial about creating the perfect cut crease could take hours between the preparation, execution, and editing. "When it comes to the business of influencing," she said, "looks can be deceiving."

Based on the size of the conference, she guessed that she'd at least double her social media following. She stayed for pictures after her speech, positioning the selfie mount next to a fan that gently blew her hair behind her. As the last woman in line stood next to Melissa, the mount fell from the wall.

"I'm so sorry," she said as she picked the phone up off of the ground and handed it back. "Let me take one on my phone, and I'll tag you on Instagram." The woman seemed pleased as she tousled her permed hair and blew a kiss to her and Melissa's image on the phone's screen.

"You're an inspiration," the woman said. Melissa smiled, winked, and posted the picture, then warmed under the first blanket of likes.

⁂

When Melissa touched down in Reno, she got a message from Mikael asking when he could meet her in person. She responded as she walked toward baggage claim: "The sweetest things in life are worth waiting for." As with the men who preceded and would follow Mikael, her interest came on quick and disappeared just as quickly. But she liked knowing that Mikael would be there if she needed him, a chocolate bar she kept hidden away in the back of the pantry. She edited his contact information in her phone, changing his name to a random assortment of characters without seeing what the end product was. That way, she could keep his number, but wouldn't be tempted to track it down when her self-sabotaging impulses caught her awake in the middle of the night.

As she looked for the navy-blue suitcase marked as her own by a pale pink ribbon on the handle, someone came up behind her and asked, "Is this my color?" Andrew was holding her bag up so that the pink ribbon was set against his jaw.

"You scared the shit out of me!" she said and almost snatched the luggage from his arms before gesturing for him to roll it alongside them. She kissed him on the cheek and said she wanted to get something to eat before beginning the four-hour drive to Elko to see her father. She asked Andrew to choose the restaurant, and he chose incorrectly.

Lucy's Bar and Grill hardly had anything she could eat. Inside, the air was thick with smoke curling off the grill, which was caked in layers of blackened grease. They seated themselves, as the sign posted beneath the cash register instructed.

The booth cushion let out a hiss of air as Melissa adjusted her sundress so that the backs of her thighs wouldn't stick to the seat when she stood up. When she ordered, the number of modifications she requested made Andrew squirm, but she knew that he wouldn't say anything. The one time he had commented on this habit, she hadn't ordered anything at all.

"Just the tuna melt for me," he said, sharing a look of camaraderie with the waiter before adding, "just as it comes." Andrew complimented her hair, which looked even shinier than usual after she'd done an avocado hair mask. Then, he complimented her makeup, specifically the evenness of her winged eyeliner. Back when they'd first met at the gym—her on the elliptical, him on the indoor rower—she'd sent him links to her three most popular hair and makeup tutorials. Now, he had the language to sincerely discuss what she did. He approached her work with reverence, as if she were an aesthetic sorceress.

Melissa picked at the chicken cut into neat cubes atop her salad for a few minutes before bringing up the home loan.

"I was thinking about the loan," she said. Andrew set down his fork and leaned forward.

"You never sent me that statement."

"You know how busy I am at those expos. I've already picked up another 500 followers." She began to take out her phone as proof.

"The loan," he redirected.

"Yeah. I think maybe I should apply for the loan by myself. Your credit is still terrible from all that credit card debt and those late payments."

"I've already talked to that lady at the bank. She said it's better to have two full-time incomes than one," he said, wiping his face using the checkered napkin, missing the mayonnaise that needed wiping.

"I wouldn't call your current job full time. Would you?"

"It's temporary. They told me that as soon as new construction starts at the Western Winds development, they'll put me back on full time. You know that."

She resisted the urge to clarify that "they" actually meant his father, who owned Quartz Construction. Because his father owned the company, Andrew was able to work as a foreman on projects that he was unqualified to lead.

"It makes the most sense for me to be the one on the loan. I think we can both still be on the title to the house," she offered, then regretted. What if he had one of his tantrums again that ended with him buying another ATV or paddleboard? She imagined him signing his name on the closing documents, his pen carrying the weight of a mafioso's anvil that'd sink her independence to the bottom of a lake. "Why don't we talk to my dad about it when we get there? He knows a lot about this kind of thing."

When the waiter delivered the bill, Andrew snatched it from his hands. He then shuffled through the credit cards in his wallet before selecting a black card showcasing the Raiders logo.

"Thanks for lunch," Melissa said.

"Of course." When they got into the car, Melissa let the quiet envelop her as she and Andrew engaged in a passive aggressive bout of minor adjustments: increased temperatures, rolled down windows, changed radio stations. By the time they arrived in Elko, they'd only spoken two phrases aloud, both independently directed at the gas station cashier in Winnemucca.

⁂

Melissa's mother greeted them before they knocked on the door. She was wearing the powder blue cashmere sweater Melissa had bought her for Mother's Day; she always wore it when Melissa came to visit.

"How was the drive?" her mother asked. The predictability of this question was a comfort to Melissa, as was the knowledge that nothing in the house she'd grown up in had changed. The upright piano still stood in the corner of the living room; two paintings of greener landscapes than the desert they knew hung above it.

"Nothing exciting to report," Melissa said. She reached for Andrew's hand, but he was now standing farther away from her than she'd thought.

"I saw a car with the front end smashed in on the side of the road while she was sleeping," Andrew added to the report. "Can I get a glass of water? Someone drank all of mine on the drive."

"Dad's in his usual spot," Melissa's mother said as she filled a glass from the tap. Both of Melissa's parents referred to their spouse without a possessive adjective, which Melissa disliked. Every time her parents said "mom" or "dad," she was reminded of her parents' parents, who were all now buried in the cemetery behind the Dairy Queen. Cancer had poisoned all the roots of her family tree.

Melissa and Andrew walked to the living room, Andrew leading the way. Her father was sleeping, and Andrew's step on the creakiest board in the room woke him before Melissa could intervene.

"Just checking out the view behind my eyelids," her father said, folding his hands atop the concave stomach that used to dip down over his waistband.

"Sounds beautiful," Melissa said.

"Mr. Brenner," Andrew said as he shook her father's hand. He did this every time they visited, and though she could tell her father appreciated the respectful gesture, it always made her feel like Andrew was playing grown-up.

Her father looked healthier this visit. His cheeks seemed fuller, and she allowed herself to hope that his condition was improving despite the most recent results from the oncologist.

"How's business?" her father asked. She began to answer, but Andrew spoke over her.

"Business has been slow. I don't know if Mel told you, but they're going to put me back to full time once they start the new subdivision south of town."

"Did you see the new development off I-80 when you drove in? Summerview, Springheights, something like that. I swear they put that whole neighborhood up in less than a month. Strong winds could knock the whole thing over easier than the big bad wolf."

"We're using higher quality materials than most," Andrew said.

"And yours, Melissa? Mom showed me your most recent video on how to mix all of the different shades to change the shape of your face. I've never seen anything like it," Melissa's father said, beaming.

"That's my subtle take on contouring," Melissa clarified through a laugh. "You don't need any contouring, Dad. You have really nice cheekbones."

Melissa's father sucked in his cheeks, which revealed too much of the skeletal structure shallowly concealed by his skin. Her mother emerged from the bedroom wearing a familiar western button-down she'd gotten at Sheplers when Melissa was younger.

"Are we ready for some poetry?" she asked, tipping her hat. "I already got our tickets to see Bart the Bard, Dad's favorite."

"Wouldn't miss it!" Andrew said. He was from the Bay Area, and he loved the novelty of the cowboy poetry festival. There was a time when Melissa liked it, too. But now, she felt like an imposter. The year before, she'd seen her high school boyfriend Isaac after the Lazy Susans performed, and he'd said she looked like she was high maintenance now, said he was sorry to see another girl move away and come back with her powdered nose up in the air. She was surprised by the accusation, but more surprised that it hurt. She'd mumbled her way through an insult about his penis, though they'd never slept together, and then had to run to the bathroom to cry and reapply mascara.

After sitting down next to her father, she got a text from a contact listed as *slkjdfis*, which she recognized as Mikael based on the preview that said "pics?" She rushed down the hallway, claiming that she needed to charge her phone. From the safety of her light purple bedroom, she deleted the text and blocked the number, then permitted herself a moment to savor the adrenaline rush before returning to the living room.

"Andrew got me straight from the airport, so I don't have anything to wear that would look right," Melissa said. She knew the event was this weekend. It was always the same time in January, and her parents looked forward to it every year. She'd chosen not to pack the right clothes.

"Lord knows I have plenty, though they'll be big on you now, twiggy as you've gotten." Her mother wrapped her arm around Melissa's waist and led her to the bedroom to pick something out.

"You're an autumn, so you've always looked good in red," her mother said as she picked two shirts from her dresser. The smell of mothballs reminded Melissa that she'd need to set up her diffuser in her room before they left for the show. She changed into the first shirt, awaiting her mother's accusation that she'd lost too much weight, but it didn't come. Instead, she said that Melissa looked strong and fit.

Her mother dropped her normally booming voice down to a whisper. "And how is everything going with Andrew? Still looking to buy a house?"

"I am," Melissa said as she picked up a tube of her mother's lipstick from a glass dish on the dresser, twisted the bottom to make the pointed tip rise and fall.

"Well, you need to buy it together," her mother said. Her father and Andrew were laughing in the living room. Her mother spoke even more softly when she added, "You're married now," as if it was a salacious piece of gossip Melissa hadn't heard.

"I'm making money with Babelicious, Mom. Like real money."

"That one looks nice," her mother said. After some back-and-forth, Melissa got permission to give her mother the signature "Babelicious Five-Minute Face"—concealer, mascara, highlighter, blush, and a swipe of lip gloss—even though she didn't usually wear makeup. They stood in the mirror to survey the results, and Melissa liked seeing how similar their features were, her mother a welcome preview into what she would look like in twenty-five years.

⁂

On the drive to the poetry performance, Melissa tended to her digital tasks, replying to emails, posting to her social media accounts, responding to comments on her YouTube channel (addressing any comments accompanied by a thumbs down first). Andrew reached for her hand, the one holding her phone, which was how he requested that she put it away. She conceded because she'd finished what she needed to finish.

"Remember the Carlsons out on Foothill, Mel?" her father asked. How could she forget? They were the ones who let her ride a mare named Sweets that, despite her name, bucked Melissa off moments after she squeezed her boots into the stirrups. The kids were nice even though they were richer than most students in Melissa's high school.

"Yeah, Joy was a year under me. Isn't their house near here?"

"That's right," her father said. "Joy lost her baby last month. Might be nice for you to go visit her while you're in town."

Melissa thought of their child development class in high school. Joy was the only one who was able to figure out a way to quiet the doll that approximated an infant baby at night. Melissa always dreaded this part of the visit, where her parents delivered news of any local tragedies. If she wanted to keep up with that news, she wouldn't have unfriended and unfollowed all of the people she'd grown up with.

When they pulled up to the Western Folklife Center, limited parking prompted her father to drop his three passengers off in front of the building. Melissa offered to stay with her father so that she could walk with him. He brushed off the offer and asked that she save him a seat as he handed her mother the tickets.

Melissa felt thankful that she fit in wearing her mother's red shirt, even if the bold red lipstick she'd chosen to go with it made her stick out a little. She recognized some of her old teachers, one of the cashiers at Albertsons, and a few of the people she went to school with, but the place was packed with tourists. Given the choice between the two, she realized that she'd prefer to be known as a local and was relieved when former classmate and fellow theater nerd Stacy Gilbert waved at her. Stacy had one baby on her hip and was holding the hand of a little girl who had her same black curls and long eyelashes.

Andrew had rushed to the bar to get them drinks when they'd arrived; he always liked an audience when he delivered hers unprompted. He handed her a whiskey and Diet Coke as she caught up with Stacy.

"Have you met my husband, Andrew?" Melissa rarely said the word "husband" aloud, and was surprised by the reassuring power of it, like stepping from a wobbly dock to a rocky shore.

"Nice to meet you," Stacy said, readjusting her baby from one hip to the other. Andrew pushed his hair out of his eyes and his lips pulled back to reveal his perfect smile created by four years of metal brackets pushing and pulling his teeth around. In the imagined competition held between the members of her graduating class, Melissa was winning. But then Stacy's husband appeared, his perfect smile the product of good genes. Melissa wished that Andrew's shirt was a little tighter to show the curve of his bicep, the V of his strong shoulders to sculpted waist.

Melissa felt her shoulders slouch. Seeing Isaac and realizing he'd married Stacy made her body fold in on itself, a display of self-conscious origami. Melissa finished her drink in two determined gulps, and Andrew dutifully retrieved another one, and then another one, and then another one after that. He liked when she drank a lot; it made her perform jealousy, wrapping her arms around Andrew's middle as soon as another girl came within shouting distance. It also made him into the caretaker and her into the one who needed taking care of.

Isaac's face fell as he and Stacy listened to Melissa talk about Babelicious. She was describing the expos, how she was getting paid to inspire other young women to pursue their dreams, how much harder her job was than people thought. They seemed to be listening intently, but Melissa soon noticed that they were leaning in because they couldn't understand her slurred speech set against the din of the hall.

"We'd better take our seats. The show's going to start soon." Aside from his initial wave, this was the only communication Isaac had had with Melissa.

Melissa pulled out her phone and saw that she had five new texts from *slkjdfis*. When had she unblocked Mikael's number? She tried to throw the phone back into her purse before Andrew saw, but it was too late. He was already staring straight ahead, unblinking.

As always, Bart the Bard was great, a real showman like her father said. He did a duet with a spoons player and sang a song about some man's terrible wife whose last attempt at cooking steak tasted more like the sole of a boot than a tenderloin filet. Melissa clapped wildly, shouted *wooooo* so loud that half of the audience members in front of her turned around.

"Stacy thinks you're hot. I can tell," she whisper-yelled to Andrew. He nodded, then handed her a bottle of water her mother had passed him. "I'll do all the loan stuff tomorrow. We can do it together." He nodded again. On the way outside, Melissa tried to think of what she'd say to Andrew. When she inspected his expression in profile—molars clenched, mouth a flat line—he seemed like he was choosing to be fine.

"If it isn't my biggest fan," someone leaning against a fence post said. With some effort, Melissa focused her eyes until the two men in front of her solidified into one complete picture of Bart the Bard. "I heard you cheering," he said in between drags from his cigarette. Outside, the wind blew in a crispy frost, and the stars shone bright. Everything felt sharp, too sharp against the blurry edges of her drunkenness. She considered getting his autograph for her father but didn't. In the distance, she saw her father turn on the heel of his boot and smile at her. Even through the smile, he looked tired, whatever fullness she'd seen in his cheeks now gone. A short walk to the truck left her father doubled over in a coughing fit, reaching to his side mirror for support.

"Those'll kill you," she called out to Bart.

"There are worse ways to go," he said, stomping out the cigarette before it was spent.

On the way home, Melissa read an onslaught of comments on the convention photo where she'd tagged the Lavish Selfie Mounts. People were complaining that the mounts couldn't stick to any surfaces, not even the mirror, and they wanted their money back. The light was also harsh, they reported. Worse even than fluorescent overhead lights. She scrolled past a comment that read "MADE IN CHINA SHIT IS JUST AS FAKE AS YOU," and her eyes stung, threatening tears. She deleted the post, replaced it with one she'd taken with her mother that night, and captioned it "Copy/paste."

A DM came in from someone with the username of Devilmakesthree. A man's grainy selfie accompanied a message that read, "I'll show you mine if you show me yours." He'd taken the picture in a bathroom mirror soiled by droplets of dried toothpaste, a shower curtain adorned with a map of the United States serving as the backdrop. He was skinny enough so that the faint outline of his sternum was visible. His blond beard was shaped to a point, like an arrow about to pierce the heart tattooed on his pale chest. Melissa laughed at the picture and the proposition, then showed it to Andrew, who laughed louder.

"What a pussy," he said. Melissa saw her father's expression in the rearview mirror, the same one he made when adults swore in the presence of children, and wished she hadn't shown the picture to Andrew. She longed for the comforts of home: her mother's cheesy toast, her father's running commentary during the 5:00 news, the thick wool blanket on the couch, the soft yellow light cast from the lamp on her nightstand.

She was thrown from her reverie when her father slammed on the brakes. The sound of locked tires on asphalt was a screechy growl. Andrew's stiff arm across Melissa's chest acted as a second seatbelt. Before asking why her father had stopped on the two-lane highway, she saw the answer standing over the road's dashed yellow lines—a deer staring straight into the truck's grill. The moon shone like a spotlight on the scene before it was winked out by a dark cloud. Melissa felt as if her heart were beating in her throat.

"Shit!" Her mother put her hand on her father's shoulder. "They always come out of nowhere." Melissa felt something like anger rising in her. Her father shouldn't even be the one driving. He was too sick to do the things he once did so easily.

"Did you hit her?" Melissa asked. She watched as the deer walked off the road. She thought it was limping, but then its movements seemed surer, the trot of a victory lap.

"No. I thought I'd clipped her tail end, but she looks okay," her father said. He tightened his grip on the steering wheel, and her mother tightened her grip on her father's hand. Melissa's heart rate slowed as her father drove on, and she watched the deer break into a run before disappearing past the hillside. It kept running even after the darkness had swallowed it up.

7

TWICE-EXCEPTIONAL

Staff List <staff-l@west-academy.com> on behalf of Mora, Gus
Tue 1/5/2019 3:18 p.m.
Subject: Welcome back!

Hello everyone,

I hope you're excited for another great semester; this time of year always makes me feel a renewed sense of hope, though truth be told, I've already abandoned the New Year's resolutions that Jean made for me. If you see me drinking coffee, don't tell her. I'm supposed to be off of caffeine until the summer, but my morning java will not be a martyr in her new war on vice.

While you were enjoying some well-deserved rest, the admin team and I have been working hard to ensure that our students have a wonderfully enriching semester here at the West Academy. We have a packed schedule of guest speakers and college recruiters who are already champing at the bit to have our brilliant students attend their respective institutions. I'm especially looking forward to a talk by Dr. Kent Li about recent developments in robotic-assisted surgery. With any luck, he might volunteer some time to see our robotics team's creation, which has secured them a spot at regionals. The competition will be live streamed, and I can't wait to cheer our BattleBot team on.

Speaking of our students' accomplishments, I saw Priyanka's parents at the Winterfest fundraiser, and they said that Priyanka has been extended an invitation to the White House to commend her for developing a wildfire preparedness program last summer after her family lost their vacation home to a fire in Sonoma. If you remember her older brother Visna (class of 2014), he graduated from Stanford last spring and developed an app to help expand the reach of Priyanka's program.

I hope you were able to enjoy your winter break (and maybe even hit the Sierra slopes)! Jean and I took our annual trip to the Monterey Bay Aquarium, and the highlight for the boys was petting a manta ray. Jackson still can't stop talking about it, and Ash says he now wants to be a marine biologist. Hopefully some of you on the science team can disabuse him of the notion that this field is all animal petting and ocean exploring. In between an otter feeding and a sandbar shark viewing, I was able to fit in a meeting with the head of the Bechtel Family Center for Ocean Education and Leadership. I'm optimistic that we will be able to set up a partnership with them for the students who are interested in ocean conservation, and I already have some students in mind who would be a perfect fit.

A new semester also means a new start for some of our students who had to go through our grade recovery camp over break. For those of you who are new to the team, remember that our students are very grade motivated, so they will hound you for detailed grading rubrics and will make sure that their report cards aren't blemished by anything but a column of beautifully pointed As. Thank you to those of you who have been working with them on essays, academic support, and extracurricular activities to help guide them back to the path that leads to their admission into their top college choices.

I hope to see all of you at the welcome back brunch that our Parent Support Team is putting together. I know that I personally look forward every year to Mrs. Chen's homemade cinnamon rolls!

Finally, I have already fielded several questions about Ms. Miller's abrupt departure. I hope you understand that there are two sides to every story, and though I cannot discuss our side here, please know that our decisions are always made with our students in mind. Do reach out to the admin team if you have any concerns you would like to talk through. I know such changes in staffing can be disconcerting, but take comfort in the fact that you all continue to be valued members of the West Academy family.

Warmest regards,
Principal Mora

***

Staff List <staff-l@west-academy.com> on behalf of Nichols, William
Subject: re: Welcome back!
Tue 1/5/2019 3:19 p.m.

Woohoo! Go Priyanka! And I guess I'll be the one to crush Ash's dreams. Ever since I implemented a flipped classroom model so that I could cover a year's worth of content in one semester, I'm informally known as the "Dream Crusher," according to some of the kids in my advanced bio class.

I was planning on swinging by your office later, but I figured before then, I'd say it here. I'm calling dibs on Sandra's classroom! I've been in this closet-turned-classroom for two years, which is two years too long, and I think I've earned the right to some daylight. Someone else is welcome to those yoga balls she had. I don't need anything else that encourages the kids to bounce around my classroom.

See you all at the brunch. I'll bring the coffee since that was sorely missed last year. Don't worry—my lips are sealed.

—Will
William Nichols, PhD
Biology Instructor
West Academy

⁂

Staff List <staff-l@west-academy.com> on behalf of Smith, Eliza
Subject: re: re: Welcome back!
Tue 1/5/2019 3:36 p.m.

It's so nice to be back! As with every break, I couldn't wait for it throughout the fall and then missed the kids so much once it started that I couldn't wait for it to end ☺. Before they return, I want to remind you of our new mental health advocacy program. Many of our students ranked their feelings of stress as a 10 on a scale of 1 to 10 on our student satisfaction surveys at the end of last semester. Poor Darwish even reported digestion issues that his parents said "only seem to come up when he talks about his physics homework." He has worse heartburn than someone quadruple his age!

You can help our kids by spreading the word about our new meditation corner and the Dog Daze we'll have around midterms when we bring in some shelter pups to ease our hardworking kids' anxiety!

You are still welcome—and encouraged!—to maintain the academic rigor of your classes; after all, gifted students need to be challenged or they will disengage and will not benefit from the focused attention and time we invest in each and every one of them. We trust all of our teachers to craft a curriculum that suits students' needs, and we would rather not begin doing observations and policing you, but we are willing to take that step if needed.

On a more concerning note, I have also gotten word about some academic integrity issues from one of my little birdies, often from students who are unwilling to ask for late work extensions. You can get a *plagiarismcheck.com* login from me if you do not already utilize this service. We are not just teaching our kiddos how to solve functions or how to apply the laws of physics. We are also teaching them how to be decent people, so it's important that we all nip this problem in the bud. Our students should all embody West Academy's values: *Integrity, Excellence, Ambition.*

Also of concern—on the survey one student and several parents also voiced their concerns about some of our humanities instructors' curricular materials, including assignments asking students to think about their "privilege." This is a reminder to be extra cautious when it comes to keeping your politics out of the classroom.

Finally, college application decisions are right around the corner. I ask that you are cognizant of the kids' mental states. Many of them will stay home with their families to await the results, and Principal Mora and I have decided not to intervene with this practice, as part of it may be cultural. These students' absences will be listed as "excused" in PowerSchool.

See you in the soon-to-be-full hallways!
Eliza Smith, MSW
College Counselor, West Academy

The content of this email is confidential and intended for the recipient specified in message only. It is strictly forbidden to share any part of this message with any third party, without a written consent of the sender.

Staff List <staff-l@west-academy.com> on behalf of Cooper, Ana
Subject: re: re: re: Welcome back!
Tue 1/5/2019 3:38 p.m.

Welcome back, everyone! I want to take the time to round out the admin's side of the story since Gus has to be more diplomatic than I do.

The relevant bit: we may not have actual pen-on-paper job descriptions, but it is still expected that you fulfill all of your duties in order to best serve our students. Ms. Miller was no longer able to meet the expectations for a West Academy instructor. While you are all valuable members, it is worth noting that there is a long list of public-school teachers who are dying to fill your shoes as you stand in front of your classes and, as the adage goes, learn more from our students than they may learn from you.

Gus and I have talked about it, and we think the best next step will be to hire a teacher who I have personally vetted. I've decided on my friend Liz who is currently a history teacher. However, she reads a lot, and I am confident that she'll be more than capable of teaching English. I have already provided her with a curriculum that I purchased, and she's excited to teach what should be taught in a core English class. We won't have to worry about her assigning readings that'll have our kiddos switching their gender identity or trying to fight "the man" in the form of salty comment cards in our suggestions box by the Zen Den.

While Lydia is the one who deals with payroll, insurance, and other HR-type stuff, Gus and I also discussed me continuing to take on more administrative roles in addition to teaching health (as if I needed to add any more hours to my 60-hour work weeks). So, if you are concerned about your position here, please come see me first.

Be well!
Ana

"Kids don't remember what you try to teach them. They remember what you are." —Jim Henson

Ana Cooper
Head of Personnel/Instructor
West Academy

[Draft] Staff List <staff-l@west-academy.com> on behalf of Bradford, Erica
Subject: re: re: re: re: Welcome back!

If no one else will say it, I will. This is horrible! We're all expected to carry on like normal and no one can even talk about Sandy like she's some kind of boogeyman. She was here for years, like way longer than most of the other teachers (and twice as long as you, Will)! I'm sorry, but this is not how you run a school! We're not all disposable, and we're not dumb. Neither are the kids. They'll smell whatever scheme you've been cooking up the moment they walk through the doors. Two sides to every story my ass.

[Draft saved at 3:40 p.m.]

Erica Bradford (wa Staff) 3:42 p.m.
Do you know what you're going to say to the kids? They loved Sandy's class. And think of how many of them ate lunch in there with her. And who's going to take over all of the clubs she was an advisor for? I'd take them on, but I'm slammed with my SAT prep side gig since Tom lost his job.

Leonora Morgan (WA Staff) has entered privacy mode

Leonora Morgan (wa Staff) 3:43 p.m.
I know!!!!

It's all kind of bullshit, right?!

Soon, they're going to have Will teaching my AmLit class. When was the last time he read a book?? Like a whole book. I should've gotten a bogus online doctorate in ed like him so I could pretend to be the authority on everything and never worry about getting fired. And him calling dibs on her room???

Erica Bradford (wa Staff) 3:43 p.m.
Speaking of which, there have been whispers of some of the other humanities teachers joining a union before they pick us all off one by one (shhhhhhhhh) Our donors would lose their minds. I can give you an enrollment form.

Leonora Morgan (wa Staff) 3:44 p.m.
We should! Seriously. Our classes are the only ones where these kids learn how to actually be good humans.

I guess why they're called the humanities haha

Happy hour tonight?

Erica Bradford (wa Staff) 3:45 p.m.
YES PLEASEEEEEEE

Staff List <staff-l@west-academy.com> on behalf of Johnson, Tina
Subject: re: re: re: re: Welcome back!
Tue 1/5/2019 3:46 p.m.

I don't mean to change the topic too abruptly to what some might deem a more trivial matter, but I went to put my lunch in the fridge this morning and it absolutely reeked—the kind of palpable stink in cartoons where you see wavy green lines rising from a dumpster! I thought the culprit was Sandy's weird fermentation project she had going in the back of the fridge. I plugged my nose and pulled out the offending jar. Inside was a slimy disc immersed in hazy liquid, either kombucha or witches' brew, I don't know. I cleaned it out, which made me sick. Even after that, it still smelled! There were plenty of lunch boxes and coffee creamer that'd gone bad. There was even half of a rotisserie chicken! I don't want to call any current employees out, but I know a lot of you are still off carbs, so I suspect this carcass belongs to one of you.

Please remember that the cleaning fairies don't visit nightly, and this particular cleaning fairy will be leaving messes to be cleaned up by the people who make them. Like some of the students catching up over break, let's start with a clean slate, including a clean fridge!

Tina Johnson
Admissions and Records

Staff List <staff-l@west-academy.com> on behalf of Miller, Sandra
Subject: re: re: re: re: re: Welcome back!
Wed 1/6/2019 2:23 a.m.

Dear Gus,

At the beginning of break, I made the choice you asked me to make between you and my job at the academy. I see now that this was the kind of test presented in the Bible, one that doesn't have a clear lesson and is open to competing interpretations by people who are eager to be redeemed.

I foolishly waited at the hotel in Monterey for a total of 19 hours. I had packed the negligee you bought me even though it looked ridiculous, and I looked ridiculous in it, my flesh hardly contained by the network of elastic bands and lace. I had also packed more pragmatic items for the activities you'd planned: a sun hat for our day hike, binoculars for birdwatching (we might see an egret!), and my travel wine glasses for a beachside picnic. When I checked in, I had to dig back into the classics to come up with an alias: Jo March. Before, thinking up a new alias was half of the fun. But it had become a chore. I'd exhausted the list of characters from our shared summer reading list and had to go back to the books I didn't like as a student and still don't assign as a teacher.

I wonder who you'll find to take my place this semester. One week is not much time to find an instructor of the caliber that the West Academy demands. I saw Ana at the grocery store yesterday, and she pretended not to see me by suddenly becoming very invested in the ingredient list on a bag of kettle chips. I don't know why I thought it wouldn't happen to me, but I really thought I'd avoid joining the ranks of other ex-teachers, lepers whose professional failures were contagious. I considered confronting her, telling her that I saw her nearly sitting in your lap after school a few weeks back. I'd stayed late to host the first You Are Enough Affirmations session.

Anyway, when I got to the hotel room in Monterey, it was nice enough—beach themed with a real sand dollar serving as the soap dish. I checked my cell phone even though I knew that you would never contact me on that number. I tried reading a new thriller I picked up in the airport (I'm too embarrassed to even list the title here), but the words started to swirl around. I read the same passage about bank heist preparations—purchasing black masks, securing a getaway car, and devising a plan to avoid setting off the alarm—three or four times before I realized that I was only absorbing the plot points as one might an impressionist painting. I had a sense of what was happening without being able to make out any of the discrete elements.

I made all of my usual catching-up calls. My brother passed the Nevada bar and already has a job lined up at a firm, the same one you recommended when I slipped on the ice outside of my apartment and you said I should sue the property owner for negligence. That law office had the most beautiful furniture I'd ever seen. It wasn't comfortable (beautiful things rarely are), but I liked feeling the firm cushions that forced my spine into improved posture. The lawyer I met there wasn't any help, as you know. I left with an even sorer tailbone and a bill I still don't plan to pay.

I fell asleep after getting sick off of a prix fixe meal I'd curated from the room service menu. The next morning, I opened the curtains to let in the sunlight, a punishment for the previous night's overindulgences. I balled that lacy web passing as underwear into the trash, along with the bottles and disposable containers my food had come in.

The next day, I went to the aquarium, determined to enjoy myself. My parents used to take my brother and I there. He was curious like your boys, and he was always looking for answers. How could Santa possibly reach that many people in one night? Where does the rain come from? Why could we only see our dad on the weekends?

Outside, it was colder than I'd prepared for. I wrapped a shawl around my shoulders; I'd packed it because I thought it might look nice in photos during our picnic. It was too thin to keep me warm, so I tightened it around me as much as I could. It was too bright out, and I looked forward to being enveloped by the darkness of the aquarium, strolling through corridors as the ocean offered a peek at her secrets. Inside, though, it was still too bright. Red wine always gives me horrible hangovers, but I like the floaty feeling. When I drink a lot of it, I feel like I'm sprawled out on a chaise lounge on the deck of a ship—a more luxurious version of the spins. If you saw how much I drank last night, you'd accuse me of once again "showing my age."

Remember when we went up to Vancouver and you tried edibles for the first time, those nasty little brownies that were burned all the way through save the layer of THC butter that was caked to the bottom? Forty-nine-years old, and you'd never experienced the joy of letting your brain take a break for a little while. Instead, yours went into overdrive. As I laughed at that reality show about doomsday preppers, you started working on the next year's extracurricular budget, figuring out which programs to slash. I never told you this, but as you fell asleep, you made whimpering sounds like a motherless puppy.

The aquarium ticket was more expensive than I wanted to pay, even with my educator's discount. I navigated around field trip groups and families, watching as they paralleled the schools of fish darting from place to place. Many of the kids banged on the glass despite their teacher's warning that doing so was against the rules and could harm the animals. I wondered what a child's fist on glass sounded like to a fish. In the tank, someone in scuba gear waved at the kids as he tended to a pump. A stream of bubbles shot to the surface, and I realized that I'd begun holding my breath. His body then threaded through the labyrinth of kelp with such grace that it seemed that the rubber fins on his feet were part of his body. The teacher did a good job balancing her stern warnings about hitting the glass with high fives and congratulations when her students got a question right. She looked to be in her mid-twenties, about my age, and I wondered which school she worked at, which students in the group would end up at Princeton or Yale or Quartz Construction or the Sierra Nevada Rehabilitation Center. Would the boy who couldn't follow the rules end up at an Ivy League? Would he become a hedge fund manager who donated to the West Academy as generously as the Chens do every year?

The wine was still churning in my stomach, so I drank greedily from a water fountain. Surrounded by all of that moving water, I'd never been so thirsty. I left the kelp forest and followed along with the current of other visitors to the tanks that housed cephalopods. A red octopus clung to the glass, white suction cups pulsating in time with my own heartbeat. I read the plaque, which said that her name was Medusa, known for her hostile relationship with the male they'd introduced to her habitat two summers prior. This species was the first invertebrate to demonstrate individual personalities, it explained, and though Medusa didn't get off on the right arm (octopi don't have tentacles!), they were hopeful that she'd become nicer as time went on. I nearly pressed my face into the glass watching her thick hyphen of a pupil. The pupillae underneath her eye made it look like it was lined by bottom lashes.

I snapped a picture of the plaque, and the flash sent her away, a balloon of burnt orange, then plum flesh that straightened into an arrow before shooting across the tank. The photo didn't turn out.

I wandered to the jellyfish den and saw an interactive fact board for kids that quizzed them on jellyfish anatomy. A boy about Ash's age lifted up a wooden door that revealed this answer, which I read, looming behind him: "Brainless beauties—jellyfish do not have brains, but don't let their simple anatomy fool you." The boy ran to a woman, a man, and another boy with the same cowlick swooping the back of his hair into a swirl. The man tousled his hair, and the woman smoothed it back out. They all stood in front of a tank of spotted jellies, which looked like floating mushrooms from a mythical forest. Only when the man spoke out explaining that the coloration was a product of algae grown in its tissue did I realize that the perfect family silhouetted against the tank belonged to you. "It's called symbiosis. They both get something out of it."

I should have left right then, but I couldn't. I followed you all the way outside to the sea otter exhibit. I could have sworn Jean saw me there, and you stopped her from saying hello. She looked prettier than I'd remembered from the last fund-raiser. It was that night in the airport hotel that you said you were going to leave Jean as I lesson-planned for my Arthurian romance unit and you drafted emails to the textbook rep from Pearson and the young scholars' liaison from Scholastic.

Standing there as the otters batted at balls and splashed a wetsuit-clad trainer to the delight of a group of teenagers, I realized what made you so persuasive. You made me feel like a performer as I entertained you with my tricks. Listen to me recite Yeats! Watch me diagram a sentence! You made me feel like a student again, one who wanted you to think I was the brightest in my class (and not just because I once *was* the brightest student in your class).

My brother says I should be angry, says I may actually have the grounds for a wrongful termination suit, but I am not angry. With each word I type, I feel my severance from that toxic place like someone's sucking the poison from a snake-bite. But I'm sucking out the poison by myself, and it isn't leaving the best taste in my mouth. I hope that the students are always well taken care of and that, just once, you tell them that they are worthwhile people even if they go to a state school.

Even though I'm feeling better, the decision to send this was not an easy one to make. I was surprised you'd still kept me on the listserv since you were so quick to remove Grace and Deb when they "resigned" last year and the year before that, respectively, and I thought it might be a sign. I remember workshopping the email you sent out to announce Deb leaving. I was the one who added the line about there being two sides to every story and am strangely satisfied to see that it's still getting some use. Perhaps this means that you still have feelings for me, after all. Or perhaps it just slipped your mind.

Mail Delivery System <mailer-daemon@outlook.com>
Subject: Delivery Incomplete
Wed 1/6/2019 2:24 a.m.

There was a problem delivering your message to gmora@west-academy.com. See the technical details below or try resending.

8

A MALE REVUE

THE BOOMTOWN CASINO'S GRAND BALLROOM smelled like coconut oil and cigarette smoke. Kate and Araceli each had their ten fingers wrapped tenuously around a pyramid of three margaritas. Kate used the plastic cups' ridges to hold her grip and recommended that Araceli do the same. The drinks were generously filled to the brim, a fact Kate credited to Araceli's plunging neckline. Whoever said that having twins would ruin a woman's body hadn't seen Araceli in a bodycon dress. They maneuvered through rows of women, gingerly stepping over toes and shuffling around purses, until they got to their seats in the third row.

"God bless you both," Jeanette said as she reached for one cup from each of them. "Did either of you hit the ATM? I only have my card." This was not the first time Jeanette had conveniently forgotten cash, but Kate didn't mind covering her. In fact, she liked the opportunity to spend money on her as one might a kid sister who doesn't get an allowance of her own. She pulled singles from her wallet until the stack between her fingers felt thick enough and passed it to Jeanette, who beamed at what was only about twenty dollars, but looked like much more.

"Antonio laid down a strict 'look, don't touch' policy, and I'm not going to start a fight with him after he's watched the boys all night," Araceli said into her margarita.

Jeanette transferred the straw from one margarita to the other, started drinking through both straws, then pressed her fingers into her temples. She had the most inconsistent alcohol tolerance Kate had ever seen, which had contributed an air of unpredictability that hung over many of their nights downtown to either delightful or disastrous effect. Kate always tried to keep pace but lagged slightly behind in case Jeanette needed taking care of.

"Brain freeze?" Kate asked, and started using the two-straw method as well, planning to order another before the show started. "I will be looking and touching as much as I please. Dave knows better than to think I'd abide by any of his policies." The truth was Dave didn't have such a policy because he wasn't a jealous man. In the four years they'd been dating, he'd never asked about her exes or gotten miffed by other men approaching her. She did wish that just once he'd feel as jealous as she had felt at his office's Christmas party a few months prior. She'd seen his drunk coworker Sheila squeeze his shoulder and whisper something into his ear. When Kate brought it up during a wobbly walk home, Dave laughed and said that Sheila wanted help setting up her new tablet. "She's a mess," he reassured her.

The group of women behind them were laughing and talking over each other as they took pictures of themselves, reviewed the pictures, and then snapped more. The group centered around a woman in her mid-twenties—only a few years younger than Kate—wearing a white dress and a faux silk sash that read "Bride-to-Be" in loopy, sparkly cursive. Kate finished both margaritas within minutes and asked Jeanette and Araceli if they wanted another drink.

"Someone's on a mission," Araceli said to Kate and held up her still-full margarita. Araceli was the most responsible of the three.

She appeared in Kate and Jeanette's lives when they needed her most. Araceli introduced them to drying racks and properly fitting bras and rental insurance. Since graduating from college, her journey into adulthood had far outpaced theirs, and Kate could feel that the ropes of friendship that bound them were beginning to fray.

"I'll take one," Jeanette said and then reached for her purse before Kate dismissed the offer to pay with a wave of her hand. As the best friend, it was her job to keep Jeanette well-supplied with liquor after each breakup, not necessarily because doing so eased her pain, but because it increased the chances of the breakup being permanent. After several drinks, Jeanette would reliably send a flurry of texts to her ex that could not be taken back.

Kate congratulated the bride-to-be seated behind them and made her way to the bar. The line was twenty women deep, and she wished she'd smuggled in her flask, but felt too old to still be doing that. She pulled out her phone and sent Dave a text, saying, "If you're looking for a good margarita, I can't say I'd recommend the bar cart outside of Boomtown's grand ballroom." He didn't respond, which she expected. He'd never gotten into texting and often called her instead of texting back, an endearing paradox given that he worked in IT. Someday, they would have kids, and the whole family would joke about what a Luddite ol' dad was.

Kate had had just enough alcohol to strike up a conversation with her fellow bar cart patrons.

"You're a braver woman than I," Kate said to the woman behind her.

"Sorry?" She looked up from her phone.

"Your stilettos. You're a braver...." Kate trailed off as she realized that the woman had returned to her phone.

She sent another text to Dave: "What are you up to?" He called her a few minutes later, and she ignored it. When they'd first started dating, Kate had found this habit of calling instead of texting insufferable, but now she felt some sadistic satisfaction in ignoring his calls. It reminded her of when she caught her first fish in the Truckee River, the satisfying tug on the line and the knowledge that she could keep the fish or throw it back in the water if she wanted to end its struggle for breath.

She ordered two shots of tequila, two beers, and a water for Araceli.

"You want me to help you carry those?" the stiletto-clad woman offered.

"No thanks. I used to wait tables, so I'm a pro." Kate lied. She had to leave the water at the bar after failing to wedge it between her bicep and ribcage.

By the time she made her way back to her seat, half of the contents of the tequila shots had sloshed out onto the gem-toned carpet. At least the confetti pattern did a good job hiding stains. Kate and Jeanette drank the sad remains of their shots as the lights went down.

The crowd was at a fever pitch until a man's silhouette appeared behind a screen, and a reverent hush came over the audience. Music blasted through the speakers perched up in the visible stage rigging. The thuds of bass made Kate feel woozy. She sipped her beer, hoping it might settle her stomach, but knowing it wouldn't, and joined Jeanette and Araceli in a harmonized *wooo*. She imagined herself and the women around her as a pod of bottlenose dolphins, whistling to their potential mates. Hadn't she read something about how dolphin mothers use a kind of baby talk with their calves? In seeing the dearth of search results for the prompt of "bttlenis dlphon mothrr sond" in her phone's browser, she realized that she was drunker than she'd thought. She closed one eye to better focus and correct the typos before Araceli suggested she put her phone away.

Soon, the silhouette on stage was joined by more silhouettes that started pelvic thrusting in alternating directions. All three women laughed as the men emerged from behind the screen, and Kate mentally stored away details—the "Take it off!" heckles, the jazz cover of Ginuwine's "Pony," the blond dancer's crooked barbed wire tattoo—to tell Dave when he came to pick her up. One of the women from the bachelorette party behind them handed forward a flask, and Kate took a big gulp of what turned out to be gin. She wished she'd sniffed it first. Gin was the only liquor that'd ever made her black out, but given that she was about to be stuffing one-dollar bills into a stranger's waistband, she figured letting some of the memories go hazy around the edges wouldn't be such a bad thing.

The screen lifted, and all eight of the men began their first routine. They ripped off their button-down flannel shirts and picked up their cowboy hats from the front of the stage. Two men had a mock shoot-out that ended in one of them dramatically tumbling to the ground and then doing the worm to the other side of the stage. Kate fumbled with her phone and tried to take a video despite the many warnings that people who took photos or videos could be kicked out.

"I paid twenty-five bucks for this. I can document what I want," she mumbled to some invisible security guard. She was able to catch the last few seconds of the man doing the worm before the lights went down again.

"You're not allowed to take video," Araceli said, sipping her now melted margarita.

"I don't care!" Kate looked around her shoulder to make sure she'd gotten away with it.

The next number was beach-themed, and the men danced around the stage wearing floral-printed board shorts, which—much to the audience's delight—were torn away to reveal floral-printed

Speedos. Kate preferred when their legs were covered up, though. Their tans extended to their mankini lines, which made her visualize them laying in tanning beds or standing in spray tanning huts. Kate had given up on waxing, tanning, and even more basic forms of upkeep one year into her relationship with Dave, which he hadn't seemed to notice.

The themes of the next few songs were unclear, and Kate couldn't tell if she was wasted or if the acts weren't supposed to make sense. Some dancers were dressed as shirtless firemen; others were leather-vested bikers. No matter what the costume was, they all had one characteristic in common—their midsections and armpits were completely hairless, and the lack of hair made them look like muscular reptiles.

"Do you think they take steroids?" Jeanette asked in between cheers. "Eddy took them in college, but he never got in trouble for it."

"Probably. You don't get a body like that from Pilates. And don't talk about Eddy. This ballroom is hereby declared an Eddy-free zone." Kate gently patted Jeanette's shoulder. Hopefully, this night would not end in tears. "Which one would you pick?" Kate asked first to Jeanette and then to Araceli. They argued about who the best one was based on their dancing ability and physique.

"I feel like that one could break me in two," Jeanette said. Kate preferred the dancer who hadn't quite nailed the choreography; she was always rooting for the underdogs. Like Dave. He was nearly a foot shorter than his two older brothers and had soft, sloped shoulders. His mother introduced him as the runt of her litter when Kate had first met his family three Thanksgivings prior. Kate's favorite dancer tripped over a cowboy hat on the ground, which ruined whatever sense of rhythm he had before.

She often imagined what she and Dave's first dance might look like at their wedding, both of them stepping on each other's toes and the guests smiling, agreeing that these two klutzes made the perfect match. "A Jack for every Jill," she imagined her Uncle Kent saying.

Kate looked around to see if she could spot any men in the audience and couldn't find a single one aside from the three Boomtown employees who stood guard in the back. The ballroom was small, hardly warranting the descriptor of "grand," and only sat about two hundred people. Kate pulled out her ticket to check if men weren't allowed to come or if they just didn't want to.

She stopped digging in her purse for her ticket once she heard an announcement that Adonis Revue platinum ticket holders could make their way to the stage for their one-on-one dances. Women stampeded through the aisles, some waving their hands in the air, others stopping to pose for quick pictures.

"Get up there for a shot with your Hulk, Jeanette. They're not even checking wristbands." Kate gently pushed Jeanette toward the aisle, and Jeanette posed as Kate and Araceli took photos.

"We'll just crop those girls out," Araceli said too loudly, the second margarita apparently getting to her. A Boomtown employee led the women onto the stage in groups of five to receive their lap dances. Seeing the women in the aisle reminded Kate of when she waited in line to ride the waterslides at Wild Waters, everyone comparing their own bathing-suited bodies to the ones around them. Once Jeanette got into a seat, Kate tried taking a picture but was caught by the guard nearest the stage.

"No photographs of the dancers. One more picture and you're out!" the man admonished her, and Kate pretended not to care. She felt badly for the man, whose index finger looked to be twisted from arthritis. She reviewed the photo and though her finger had blocked most of the camera's lens, she could still make out the outline of the dancer straddling Jeanette, who sat in a metal folding chair.

"Should I send this picture to Eddy?" she asked as she rooted around Jeanette's purse to retrieve Eddy's number from her phone. She tried not to invade Jeanette's privacy too much as she pushed aside tubes of lip gloss and receipts, but couldn't help but linger on the strip of photobooth pictures of Jeanette and Eddy. No variety in their poses—just open-mouthed kissing with jaws positioned at slightly different angles. Kate looked back to Jeanette to see that she, along with the other four women seated in a row, was still receiving her lap dance and hoped that the Hulk wasn't letting her absorb anywhere near his full weight.

"Sure," Araceli said, and Kate wished she had told her not to. "Write something like 'out with the old.'"

Kate copied the number into her phone and sent the picture. She had not included any caption at all, mostly because the letters still blurred, but decided that the combined layers of mystery—unknown number, unknown shirtless man, unknown situation—might be even more powerful. "Sent!" she said as she wedged her phone under her thigh. Jeanette returned to her seat, her face a damp white sheet.

"I've never felt an actual six-pack before," Jeanette said. "Eddy was strong, but not defined like that. You should've heard the kinds of things he was whispering to me, and my dance was way longer than the others."

Kate and Araceli agreed and added that she looked really pretty under the stage lights.

"Did you see how shiny they were?" Jeanette continued. "Look. It's from body oil." She showed them her oil-slicked palm.

More women caught onto the fact that the staff members weren't checking wristbands. Eight more groups sat down for their lap dances, and Kate pitied the dancers, who were starting to look tired. Their gyrations slowed, and their faces reddened with exertion. A song started to skip; "baby" repeated over and over again, which didn't seem to affect the dancers at all, but unsettled Kate. Finally, the track finished, the lights went up, and a woman wearing jeans and a Boomtown polo shirt announced that the show was over. Adonis Revue dancers would be available to take pictures and sign T-shirts and body parts outside of the ballroom. The employee with arthritic fingers ran up the stairs and said something in her ear, and she added a correction that the audience members could no longer request to have body parts signed.

Other audience members rushed around the three women through the two sets of double doors that exited to the dancers' meet-and-greet area, the click of high heels dampened by the casino carpet. Kate made her way back to the bar cart, delivered the round of drinks to the other girls who were in the back of the line to get their tickets signed, and potentially exchange contact information with Jeanette's dancer. Kate walked to the bathroom and settled into a couch that, according to the sign above it, was reserved for breastfeeding mothers. Pretty progressive for an old, failing casino. She pulled out her phone to take a picture of the sign to send to Dave. Once the screen lit up, she saw a barrage of texts from Eddy's number.

Who is this?

Hello! Who is this?

Seriously! Who is this?!

Is that Jeanette????!

Kate decided it best that she leave Eddy hanging and smiled at the success of her plan, though the vague feeling that she shouldn't have sent the text made her stomach sour. She wondered what Dave would do if he received the same text. He would probably not respond or even remember it until she brought it up later. Then she'd give more details about how the dancer had come onto her, and he'd say something like "lucky him," and then go to the fridge to see if there were any leftovers.

Kate reapplied her lip balm and joined in on a session of strangers validating one another while washing their hands.

"I love your lipstick," she said to an older woman. A business card appeared in the woman's hand, and Kate took it.

"I'm a Love Your Lips consultant," the woman said. "This is Berrylicious. Want to try it?"

Kate hesitated before applying a coat that extended slightly beyond the outline of her lips. She wasn't used to wearing makeup and felt like a rodeo clown. Her lips stung.

"Feel that? It's the plumping effect. That is definitely your color. We're always looking for new consultants if you're interested."

"I work full-time, but thanks for this," Kate said as she pointed to her lips using the corner of the business card.

One woman readjusted her nylons to hide a run. Another woman used her fingers to smooth the parts in between her box braids. Kate smoothed down the hairs that had begun to frizz at her own part, took a picture of herself puckering her lips, captioned it "xoxoxoxxx," sent it to Dave.

By the time Kate returned to the meet-and-greet line, Jeanette and Araceli had gotten to the front. Araceli was taking pictures of Jeanette and her dancer, his arm casually placed around her shoulder and her arm wrapped around his waist so that her hand was covering the better part of two of his ab muscles. Araceli gestured for Jeanette to move her hand so as not to obscure any of the six-pack.

"Were you wearing that shade before?" Jeanette asked.

"I forgot about that," Kate said and rubbed off the lipstick using the back of her hand. Her phone vibrated, which she assumed was Dave calling, but it was a text. The thrilling departure from his usual communication habits was diminished by the text's contents: "haha."

The three made their way to the casino floor after Araceli announced that she had about an hour left before Antonio would pick her up. They went to their favorite table game first—blackjack—and ordered more drinks from the cocktail waitress at the first opportunity.

"So, did you get his number?" Kate asked. She'd busted after mindlessly sweeping her cards against the table to hit even though she knew better. The dealer scooped up the chips and put them back in their slotted homes.

"They can't give out their personal numbers," Jeanette said defensively. "But he said he'll come find me after they're done." She stood up, as if suddenly remembering she had somewhere to be, and moved to the seat at the table that had the clearest view of the landing where people leaving the ballroom were funneling out. She alternated between looking at the ballroom exit and the direction of the front entrance.

Kate looked over at Araceli's chip stack, which was higher than Jeannette's and Kate's put together. How many hands had they played? She sent a text to Dave asking if he'd come get her, and if he stopped to pick up a hamburger on the way, she would be eternally grateful.

"No phones at the table," the dealer said, and Kate apologized.

"How are the boys doing, Araceli?" Kate asked.

"Oh, I didn't tell you two that we finally got them on the waitlist for Sierra Montessori School." She looked at her cards and flipped them over to reveal a push. "We've been trying to get them on there since before they were born."

"That's great," Kate said. "Isn't that great, Jeanette?" But Jeanette kept staring off into middle distance.

"And their third birthday is in two weeks," Araceli continued.

"Three is such a fun age," Kate said. She didn't know what made an age fun, and truthfully, her cousin Morgan's three-year-old son was an absolute terror, constantly biting other kids and using his juice boxes as water guns to shoot apple juice onto the carpet.

About twenty minutes and twenty dollars later, the cocktail waitress delivered their drinks, and Kate tipped more than she'd planned to; the crisp ones she originally got from the bank to tip the dancers stuck together.

"You can have my drink, Kate. Antonio's here," Araceli said. She hugged Jeanette before adding, "You're better off without him." Araceli left, and Kate felt a pang of jealousy. Her boyfriend, a hamburger, and her bed were a galaxy away.

She considered getting another twenty dollars' worth of chips, but as she went to put the twenty on the table, she saw Jeanette's eyes widen and knew the dancer had actually made good on his promise to find her after the show.

Kate heard yelling before she saw what was happening. People at surrounding tables stood up from their stools to see. A man was curled up on the landing, and three different security guards were pulling some crazed man off of him. Kate and Jeanette joined the rest of the crowd to inspect the scene. Once she was within a few feet of the landing, she recognized the attacker as Eddy, though his eyes were so dilated that he looked like some hideous rodent. He was swinging his arms wildly against the guards restraining him and successfully threw two of them off.

Kate had only met Eddy once, and he had seemed nice enough, even offered to pick up the tab for pizza for all three couples. He hadn't said much but gave Jeanette lots of compliments about her hair and her sweater and the fit of her jeans. Dave and Antonio kept up complimenting their respective partners until the compliment chorus sounded ridiculous. Dave's last compliment was that Kate was deceptively strong and would make a good pioneer woman. Eddy started to seem manic, blinking his eyes quickly and constantly turning to keep tabs on who entered and exited through the front door. Finally, the other two couples avoided eye contact with Eddy altogether. "Freak" was the word Antonio used to describe him. Dave, who said he would reserve judgment for now, called him "intense."

Now, Kate joined the security guards' effort to pry Eddy off of the dancer, and they pushed her out of the way.

"Stop it!" Jeanette yelled. Kate knew she was likely more of a hindrance than a help but felt she had to do something. She heard an audible crunch as Eddy got in one final kick to the man's face.

She caught a glimpse of the dancer, his nose bleeding and both eyes already swelling. He whimpered, cradled his ribs, and writhed around before he stopped moving altogether. Even with the disfiguration of his face, she could see that it wasn't the dancer that Jeanette had received her dance from. A loud buzz sounded in her ears, and she looked around for the source, but couldn't find it. The taste of beer, smoke, remorse, and guilt swirled around her mouth, and she swallowed the urge to puke.

"Stop," Jeanette repeated, quieter this time. "Eddy, you don't need to do that."

Kate reached into her purse to offer the dancer a tissue, a painkiller, or something else that could be useful, but only had antibacterial gel. She offered it to him anyway, but he didn't respond. Eddy was finally hauled off to some place deep within the bowels of the casino, and strings of profanity rang across the casino floor as he was dragged away. Everyone stared at the dancer, who was thankfully moving again. Another dancer parted the crowd and knelt beside his colleague, comforting him in hushed words. When the paramedics arrived, security guards dispersed the crowd. Kate and Jeanette stood near the front doors and watched as the dancer was loaded into the ambulance. The normal soundscape of the casino—hundreds of competing slot machine theme songs and conversations—had returned. Kate got a voicemail from Dave saying that he was parked in valet and had picked up a late-night snack for her.

"We'll give you a ride home," Kate said, and laced her arm through the gap between Jeanette's elbow and her waist. "I have to tell you that this is my fault. I texted him a picture of you during that dance."

Jeanette started to cry. "I know. Eddy texted me, and I told him I was here."

Kate pulled her arm away, and she felt a wave of relief as she began to transfer the blame for what had happened from herself to Jeanette.

"What the fuck is wrong with him?"

"I guess he's more protective of me than I thought," Jeanette said.

Kate left Jeanette standing alone by the doors and found Dave waiting in the valet. He removed the fast-food paper bag from the passenger seat to make space for her and clicked on the overhead light between them.

"You look pale," he said.

"Too much gin." Maybe she would tell him about the fight when she sobered up. She'd say that she was just trying to be a good friend, trying to make Eddy see what he'd missed out on, but that it wasn't enough for Jeanette. She'd thank Dave for being kind and safe and for rubbing her feet when she didn't feel well. She'd tell him he could set up Sheila's tablet if she asked him to again because that would be a nice thing to do.

"They were out of strawberry, so I got chocolate instead." He handed her a milkshake, and she pressed it against her face, which felt flush.

Kate thanked him and rested her head on his pillow-soft shoulder. She watched as the casino sign's lights blinked on and off in a pattern of organized chaos. Even behind closed eyelids, she could still feel the lights pulse.

9

ARTIFACTS WORTH SAVING

THE NIGHT BEFORE ELSA LEFT, she and her husband, Landon, discussed the difference between azure and powder bluc. Decisions had to be finalized before she left to do archeological fieldwork in Italy: Shaker style or beadboard cabinets, solid surface or granite countertop. Landon knew that Elsa couldn't quite get herself to care about the remodel. He opened up a catalog he'd picked up for window coverings to the first page he'd dog-eared, and she nodded when he presented the options.

"Honestly, I don't know if it's worth it to get the Roman shades," Landon said, pointing to the glossy catalog page.

"Thanks for being honest." Elsa smiled, but didn't look up from the article she was reading.

"I want to be all moved in before you get back in July."

"You know it's not really my thing."

"What's not your thing?" Landon closed the catalog. "Being moved in? Giving a shit about our new house?"

"Both, I guess." If Elsa was surprised to hear Landon departing from his no-swear policy, she didn't show it. "And who names these colors anyway? Dignity blue? As opposed to Dishonorable Blue?" She picked up the paint swatch and shook her head.

The conversation ended like the ones before it had. Elsa started talking about the dig site and the big-brained people she'd be working with. Landon gave up on eliciting design decisions from her and motioned for her to sit on his lap. The 8,500-year-old remains of someone the excavation team was calling "Witch Girl" were more interesting than paint color or wall texture anyway.

"I still can't believe Dr. Cline asked for me specifically." Elsa sat in his lap and reached for her article. "This is huge for me. If the radiocarbon dating pegs her before the fourteenth century, that means my theory about there being witch trials before Val Camonica is right."

"What do they think happened to her?" Landon wrapped his arms around Elsa's middle.

"They burned and buried her before stacking some rocks on top."

"Well, that's one way to go."

She stood up and didn't apologize after realizing she'd smashed Landon's toe beneath her rubber-soled slipper. The two slept as crescents that curved away from one another. In the middle of the night, Landon tried to put his arm around Elsa, but she twisted away from him. He slept for an hour or two before getting up, brewing a cup of coffee, and revisiting the window-covering catalog.

In the morning, Landon drove Elsa to the airport and she gave him a surprisingly wet kiss before getting out of the car.

"Pick whatever you want for the house. There's still plenty of money in the joint account for porcelain tile or dishonorable blue paint or whatever else you decide on," she said and kissed him again. "You know it'll be tough to get in touch, but I'll call when I can."

"Yeah, yeah. There goes my wife solving the greatest archeological mysteries of our time." Landon pulled out her bags and set them neatly beside one another on the curb. It didn't look like she'd packed enough to last six weeks, but Landon didn't say anything.

He tried to kiss her one last time on the back of her head as she started to walk toward the airport's entrance, but she was already too far away.

When Landon returned to the apartment, it didn't feel as empty he expected it to. Even though all of their possessions were boxed up, it felt bigger in a good way. Elsa's shoes were put away for once and her organic body soaps and face creams were packed into boxes. There was a time when he'd resented the fact that she expected him to pack everything up and move it while she was gone. Not to mention coordinate the remodel for the house they'd bought. But when someone's not working, it's easy to assume that they will welcome any task. It was better this way anyway. He had planned lots of little surprises for when she got back. He would frame the pictures taken at their wedding the year before and would finally open up the rest of the kitchen gadgets he'd registered for.

Their apartment was in Stead (their new homestead, they called it despite being flanked by strip malls). It was hot, and Landon took his shirt off to keep cool. It felt indecent when he saw his reflection in the window, but he'd take indecency over having a shirt stuck to his body by a sweat adhesive. He went to flip on the swamp cooler and realized that it wasn't making its usual mechanical groan. Landon and his friend Neil had installed it themselves two months prior, so he knew that it should be working fine. He flipped the switch on and off, tried flipping it to "on" one more time, and gave it a little kick before resorting to finding the user's manual.

"If this thing isn't still under warranty, we're going to have a problem. Right, Freddie?" Landon raised his eyebrows at their pet chameleon, perched on a fake tree branch in its terrarium. The lizard looked in two different directions and continued climbing the branch. If Freddie was good for one thing, it was serving as the other side of a one-sided conversation when Elsa was out doing fieldwork. Landon had surprised Elsa with the lizard on their first dating anniversary. She'd told him that she'd always had a soft spot for their curled-up tails and downward-turned mouths, which he'd made a note of in his mental list of gift ideas. He was a much better gift-giver than she was, and these days, that was about the only thing he had won in the unacknowledged game of "Who's the Better Spouse?"

Landon could feel drops of sweat dripping down the inside of his elbow as he searched for the swamp cooler's warranty and user's manual. He could picture exactly where it had been before they'd packed everything up. He kept impeccable records and regretted letting Elsa pack up the office. "Most of this stuff is mine now anyway," she'd said before throwing books and paperweights and ink cartridges all into the same box. Her rock collection had replaced his cover letter drafts; her framed doctoral degree hung where a picture he took of the Grand Canyon once had.

Sharp, small letters identified one box as "miscellaneous." Landon cut through the tape, and at first it looked promising. He found the information for their new appliances and the instructions for assembling the kitchen table they had bought online. Beneath those instructions, Landon found a box decorated with blue and brown polka dots. The corners of the box were worn away, revealing its cardboard insides.

Landon lifted off the lid and saw pictures of Elsa and her brother from when they were kids. No wonder she had shut the photo album when her mother tried to show Landon photos of baby Elsa. She was one awkward-looking kid. She wore thick glasses that extended above her eyebrows and below the plumpest parts of her cheeks. In one picture she was holding a turtle in one hand and a protractor in the other. Landon laughed. In a school picture it looked like she smiled closed-mouth to conceal her braces, and she posed with her flute. Seeing his wife as she was then made her flaws seem forgivable if not lovable. Her mismatched socks and frizzy hair suited her just as well then as her dress socks and groomed ponytail did now.

⁂

Four weeks later, Landon woke up to a call from Elsa. It was almost 10 a.m., so he tried hard to sound as if he had been awake before she called. The last thing he needed in this heat was a lecture on how he should have contacted the district again to see if any long-term substitute teaching jobs had opened up.

"Hey sweet—." He cleared his throat. "Hey sweetie. How's our friend Witch Girl doing?"

"She's been fully excavated now. First tests will run tomorrow."

"Let me know once you figure out a date for her. I want to know if you were right. You're always right when you're with me, so I don't see how this would be any different." She laughed a quiet laugh.

"Did you just get up? What time is it there?"

"Nah, just trying to fix the swamp cooler. It's almost ten here." He had given up on fixing the swamp cooler three weeks before.

"They're expecting me back, but I wanted to call you. It's worse than I thought it'd be. They could tell that the body had been burned before it was buried, but they don't know whether or not she was already dead. It was bad even by deviant burial standards. There was a brick-sized stone in her mouth, which the lead researcher told me was used to break her jaw. She was also partially dismembered. I knew about the dismemberment, but Jesus, breaking her jaw? And then leaving the stone in there?"

"You've told me about way worse things than that before. Not to say that isn't horrible, but I feel like that's the tip of the witch trial iceberg."

"I've never seen one this intact before. The bones look so small."

The phone cut out before the two could exchange I love yous. Funny, he thought. The cell phone connection seemed fine. Landon went back to the miscellaneous box. He allowed himself two pictures of little Elsa a day as a treat for fixing up the new house.

So far, he'd seen pictures of her playing her flute in marching band and posing for her prom pictures. It felt absurd, but he was jealous of the almost handsome boy who had his hand placed gingerly on Elsa's hip.

He reached the bottom of the box, and beneath a photo of Elsa doing a handstand was a thin, glossy piece of paper that had been folded in half. Landon opened it up and saw a sonogram. That was an odd thing to give to your kid, but his mother-in-law had given Elsa lots of things back that he felt a parent should keep. Before Elsa's parents moved to Palm Springs, her mother had dropped off a box that even included gifts that Elsa and her brother, Danny, had given to her as kids. There was a painting of a reindeer with Elsa's handprints for antlers and a Valentine's Day acrostic poem that spelled out M-O-M and D-A-D. But the sonogram didn't look old enough to be from when Elsa's mother was pregnant with her. A small rectangle had been clipped from the upper left-hand corner. He scanned the sonogram for Elsa's name, or a date, but he didn't need that information to piece the puzzle together.

He'd detected a slight roundness to her stomach. "Cortisol is a stress hormone, and it makes you gain weight in your stomach," she'd said when she caught him staring as she changed into her pajamas one night. He had believed her because she always had trivia like that up her sleeve, and she said it with such conviction that there was no reason to doubt her. She knew the main exports of most South American countries, the gestation period of rhesus monkeys, and the etymology of the word "Mesolithic."

And then there were the dramatic mood swings. Landon worried that she was having trouble adjusting to life living with her new husband. As his mother insisted, they'd gone the traditional route by waiting until they were married to move in together, and he worried that she didn't like having his things mixed in with her own. He knew that there was something about seeing his deodorant next to her hairspray that bothered her.

Landon couldn't tell if it was the heat or the sonogram that he still had pinched between his fingers, or a combination of both, but he felt sick. He ran to the bathroom and retched. The bathroom was dark, and he didn't turn the light on. The cold tile felt good on his feet. He splashed water on his face and let the droplets run down his cheeks instead of drying himself off.

The new house had four bedrooms, which is what he had fought for when they were house hunting.

"I don't want to start having kids and have to uproot and move once we've outgrown our house," he'd said. "Could you imagine having to move with three kids yelling at you the whole time?" The realtor had taken Landon's side, and Elsa had trouble making her case. "I at least get my own room," Elsa had said.

His sickness shifted from shocked to excited nausea, and he ran to the bedroom to get his phone. He knew that Elsa didn't do well with accusations, so he decided to lead by telling her that everything was going to be okay. He'd say that he wasn't mad that she hadn't told him, since he knew she didn't feel ready to have kids. He called twelve times but left no voicemails. Elsa was not the type to check a voicemail before calling back.

Landon looked at the sonogram again and tried to make sense of the image. It didn't look like a baby; it looked like the entrance to an oblong cave with one small sphere nestled inside.

He compared it to ones he found online to get an idea of how old the baby was, but without knowing when the image was taken, there wasn't much use trying to figure out its age. His search was interrupted by a call from Elsa. She sounded panicked.

"There's another one," Elsa said.

Landon's throat tightened. "Jesus. Twins?" He was relieved that she was the first to bring it up and worried that something had gone wrong. He'd already started to search online to see if constant crouching, long flights, inhaling dust, and other archeological work hazards could be bad for a baby.

"What? No. Another deviant burial about two kilometers from the excavation site. Luckily, they had an archeologist on site during the development of a new industrial complex."

Landon listened to her breathe, each breath its own sigh.

"I'll have everything, and I mean everything, ready by the time you get back," he finally added. "The most important thing for you to do right now is relax as much as you can, get your work done there, and come back home."

"Yes, well there's a lot of work to be done now. Anyway, they're calling for me."

Landon wondered how much more Elsa was showing now. He smiled at the thought of her cargo pants getting a little too tight around the waist. He pulled out the paint swatch and started to look at different shades of yellow for the nursery.

In the next two weeks, Landon rarely heard from Elsa—and when he did, their conversations were quickly interrupted by a faraway voice saying that Elsa was needed for something or another. She sent him a lot of emails, though, mostly articles about deviant burials, the plague, and the witch trials of Val Camonica. Learning about what she was doing made him feel closer to his wife, so he printed all of the articles out and read them carefully.

One morning, he saw an email sent after an article about the nearby burial and one about Dr. Cline being honored by the Archeological Institute of America. "I'm sorry," the subject line read. Landon expected an apology about how little Elsa had contacted him. He expected her to say that she felt badly that he was doing all of the work on the house. He expected to be relieved once he read the apology; the little pebbles of resentment that he could feel piling up inside of him would be washed away. But when he opened the email, he saw something else.

"I lost the baby." He read the four words over and over again. They looked especially cold above her signature automatically attached to her emails: *Elsa Hutchings, PhD, University of Nevada, Reno*. Without thinking, he went to the nursery to find the sonogram that he'd framed and tossed it into the trash bin next to Elsa's desk. Before calling Elsa, he fished it back out of the trash. Instead of greeting him with a hello, she answered by saying, "I'm sorry."

"Are you okay?" Panic crawled up his throat, made him choke on his words.

"I didn't know how to tell you. I wanted to do it right, buy the baby hiking boots that look like ours and surprise you when I got home. I wanted me to be the one who was ready." She was crying. It was only the second time he'd heard her cry. The other time, she hadn't been allowed to work on a project because of a torn ACL. She had seemed just on the verge of crying when he'd proposed, but they had been outside and it was hard to see her eyes behind her sunglasses.

"Are you okay?" Landon repeated. He wiped a smudge from the sonogram's frame.

"My body is fine." Her cries softened. "When I found out, it was right before I left, and I could only imagine a group of cells multiplying inside me. I couldn't see a baby that would have your eyes and my hair and your patience and my persistence. I couldn't see the day care or the little socks that look like shoes or the cloth diapers. It was just cells, and then when it was all over, it was just cells again."

"The baby would have been beautiful and smart like you. It's okay to think of it as a baby. It's okay not to. I want to reach through this phone and hold you."

"I wish you could. I love you."

Landon cried for what they had lost. After hanging up, he let what he'd learned settle into each of his cells. The crib would need to be disassembled and returned. The yellow walls painted over.

He asked Neil to come help him move a few days before Elsa would return. He'd painted the walls in the new house white and planned to hang some of their wedding photos—one of her kissing the top of his head, another of her giving the flower girl a piggyback ride—up on the east wall. The disassembled crib still sat in the corner of the room.

Neil picked up the sides of the crib and walked to the truck.

"Is this what I think it is?"

"Oh yeah, just load it up in the truck." His eyes flitted from side to side as he thought of what to say. "It was a gift from my pushy aunt. Did you ever meet my Aunt Leslie?"

Neil looked confused.

"It's a hand-me-down." Landon used the line that Elsa had whispered to him when her father had made a gross joke about what would happen on their wedding night. "Apparently, getting married means people can start telling you to procreate."

The two unloaded the rest of the boxes and drank two beers, as if they'd just been talking about sports or the weather or something else that friends talk about when they're moving boxes.

Once Neil left, Landon started to unpack the boxes but couldn't get himself to return the crib. He'd gotten such a good deal that it seemed like a shame to get rid of it. What might it look like when it was assembled, with a baby inside it? The baby might wear a blue-striped onesie and roll from side to side. Maybe she'd chew on her toes and stare up at a nautical-themed mobile. Maybe it'd be a he, and he'd try to escape once he got old enough. Landon would want to get the baby monitor that connected to your phone to prevent such an escape. Plus, Elsa liked getting the newest gadgets. He smiled thinking about what could be.

Getting ready to pick up Elsa from the airport felt like preparing for a first date. Landon put on the navy shirt he knew Elsa liked him in, brushed his teeth, dumped some crickets in Freddie's tank, and brushed his teeth again.

He was ten minutes early, but didn't want to risk her coming outside and not seeing him, so he drove in slow circles around the airport. It was hot and abnormally humid, and he blasted the AC so that it'd be more comfortable for her. He was glad that she didn't have to suffer in the hot apartment with him. The AC in their new house worked great, and he had it programmed just how Elsa liked it. She liked to be colder at night so that she woke up with a cold face and a warm body. As Landon drove in circles, he started to feel like some things he'd chosen for the house were wrong. He knew Elsa would like how he'd organized all of the spices, and that he'd gotten a comfortable couch to replace their old one. But he worried about the window treatments in their bedroom. The curtains were too dark, and she might think it felt like a cavern. He talked himself back into liking his decisions for the house after the sixth or seventh lap. Each choice had been made with Elsa in mind, and she would appreciate that.

On the fifteenth lap around, he saw Elsa's luggage before he saw her. She wore a wide-brimmed hat that she must have bought in Italy. The style of the hat clashed with the T-shirt she was wearing. As Landon got closer, he tried to see if the T-shirt fit looser than it did when Elsa had left. He stepped on the brake without realizing it. The heat rising up off of the asphalt made a mirage that made him feel like he was in a dream. He watched his wife scan the cars in front of her to find his, and he wondered what the right thing to say would be. People behind him started to honk their horns, which drew her attention. She waved, and he couldn't get himself to wave back, so he nodded instead, mouth still agape like a cartoon character.

He got out of the car to help load her bags and nearly fell over when she swung her arms around his shoulders, jumped up to wrap her legs around him. She squeezed him so tightly he could hardly catch his breath.

"Honey," he wheezed.

"I just missed you." She slid off him and put her bags in the car. "God, it's hotter than Hades here, but it's good to be back."

On the way to their house, she talked and Landon listened. Someone on the flight had gotten drunk and made her get up so he could go to the bathroom six or seven times. Dr. Cline might be leading another project, but he wouldn't know if it'd get funding until the next summer. Landon could hardly get a word in. He held tightly onto the steering wheel and accidentally cut someone off. His mind felt like it was floating somewhere outside of his body, like a passenger in the back seat.

When they got to the house, Elsa tried to slip inside first, but Landon edged her out so that he could give her the tour and describe everything he'd done.

"Nice and cool in here!" Her cheerfulness unsettled him. She kicked her shoes off by the doormat, and seeing something more of her there felt good. She rushed in front of Landon and started to explore, pulling out drawers and opening cupboards.

"What do you think?" Landon followed her as she moved from room to room in something between a walk and a skip.

"Great. Just so great." He wondered if this was her usual brand of sarcasm, but her smile seemed real. When she got to her office, he could feel her whole body sag as she spotted the crib. She nodded in its direction.

"We can get rid of it, but eventually, we might—." He tried to read her, but she didn't move, didn't blink even.

"It was just a really good deal. I can put it in the garage."

Elsa uncrossed her arms, walked to the crib, and ran her fingers along one of its slats.

"Keep it," she said. "I want to keep it."

10

THIS CONTENT IS CURRENTLY UNAVAILABLE

When I got the third and final warning from my son's day care that he had bitten another child, I blinked, said "I see," and hung up the phone. I'd just begun working as a social media content screener, and compared to the videos I'd already seen of dismembered dogs and brutal muggings, what was a little nip? How strong are baby teeth anyway?

After getting the call, I dedicated all ten minutes of my allocated wellness time to finding a new day care, one that focused on social emotional learning. The one called Kids Play! was the most promising place that fell within my monthly budget, so I sent an email to the director asking if they had any open slots. Had my ex-fiancé Noah not moved to Bristol to put an entire ocean between us, he would have objected to this place based on the name alone. Had I told him that I had a child—his child—he would have objected to much more.

My ten minutes expired too soon, and each step that brought me closer to my cubicle quickened my pulse. A man had died at work just two cubicles down, and I avoided walking past it even though the detour added valuable seconds to my route. My coworker Claire told me that it had been an hour before they realized that he'd silently passed on from a heart attack that wasn't nearly as dramatic as the movies make those out to be, that she saw the faint outline of keyboard keys imprinted in his cheek. I don't know if that's true. Still, I often had to blink away that image when I walked near that cubicle.

I counted three deep breaths before sitting in my squeaky-backed chair. At work, my hands didn't click through the videos without my brain instructing them to. I said open, open to my clenched right fist, and by that time of day, my fingernails had worn pink indentations into the fleshiest part of my palm. My finger hovered above the button on my mouse until I said click, click.

The first video had been flagged for depicting a knee surgery that may have been recorded without the patient's consent. After reviewing the video, I determined that it should not be permitted, though there wasn't a choice in the drop-down menu of reasons that quite fit. After enough of these videos were flagged, a category that suited them would be made. The video types came in waves, and the graphic surgery videos had not yet crested. Then came a series of the usual videos—flashings on city buses, *accidental* nip slips from spring breakers, clips set to copyright-protected songs. These were the easiest to categorize, and though I could have rushed through them, I didn't. Instead, I made a study of these videos, trying to identify certain patterns. For example, the men who flashed their naked bodies typically had wildly unkempt genitals that fairly earned the moniker of "junk." The spring breakers often had jewelry pierced through their belly buttons. The copyrighted songs were frequently rock ballads from the eighties or contemporary songs that continuously cycled through pop radio stations with names like Hot 104.5 or Wild 95.7.

The next video had a level of nuance that necessitated more than my immediate, almost robotic ability to categorize the videos could provide. In it, an eight- or nine-year-old girl was being fitted in a wedding gown that looked like the Disney princess costumes made of scratchy tulle. If I didn't know that it'd been flagged already by another screener, I would have allowed myself to enjoy the scene, which looked a lot like the ones I'd played out when I was a little girl, imaginative by necessity as an only child. As soon as a veil was brought over her eyes, a group of men were led into the room. She began to cry as an auctioneer rattled off prices to the men, who were now licking their lips and shouting at each other. Sweat began to collect in between my palm and the mouse beneath it. "Please not any further," I wished aloud. And with the PSA's bright white text reading, "Some little girls don't have a choice but to say 'I do,'" my wish was granted.

⁂

On my way to pick up Oliver, I listened to dream pop. A slide guitar's echoes edged out the static noise that'd been buzzing behind my eyes since I'd finished my employee training. This sound couldn't be silenced but could be disguised by music and dampened by paychecks. The day care was only three blocks from work, and the drive didn't give me enough time to prepare anything to say; even if it were longer, I wouldn't know what to prepare.

In the parking lot, another parent whose name I should have known waved at me, and I waved back, hoping that he would not interpret this as a conversational invitation. Thankfully, he continued walking to his minivan, then put whatever yarn-covered craft his daughter had made in the front seat and pretended to buckle it in. I smiled and tried hard to pull his name out of the dusty storage boxes in my mind that housed this kind of information. But no luck.

After signing in, I was led back to the group of children sitting in a circle and holding hands. Oliver was missing. Panic flashed first in my mind and then in my stomach. The first time I had lost sight of Oliver had been in a mass of bodies at the public pool down our block, and a dry heave had left the faint taste of chlorine water on the back of my tongue for the rest of the day. It turned out he'd been hiding behind the lifeguard's stand.

"Miss Emily, do you know where Oliver is?" I asked, concealing a grimace. In the journal my online therapist recommended I use, I called all of the teachers by their first name only.

Miss Emily seemed saddened by the question, and she stopped fishing plastic markers out of the crayon bin. She folded her arms and stood too close to me.

"Didn't someone call you about what happened? We had to separate Oliver from the others after today's incident." I nodded along with the explanation before Emily added in a whisper, "After he bit Lucy." She returned to her work sorting art supplies before situating herself in the kids' circle. I scanned the circle to guess which girl was Lucy, looking at all the bare arms and legs for little bruises that arced in the shape of my boy's teeth. I didn't see anything but noticed that one girl had gotten a sunburn.

I was led back to an office, all metal corners and tools to punch holes through paper, slice card stock in half, sharpen pencils to a point. This was not a place for children, but Oliver didn't seem to notice. He was sitting in a corner fitting plastic shapes into holes—all correctly.

The woman at the desk nearest me did not notice how skilled Oliver was at playing with the toy, how smart he was for only being two-and-a-half. She hardly seemed to notice that I'd walked into the room. Eventually, she put her hands together as if in prayer and asked me to pull up a chair. Oliver exclaimed "Hi mom!" But his excitement disappeared as soon as it had appeared.

"As I said on the phone—I think the line may have cut out. Sorry about that. Anyway, as I said on the phone, we will no longer be able to serve your family here." The woman refused to look at Oliver, refused to look directly at me. I thought of one of the videos I had screened earlier, the one titled "Mom leaves her kids in hot car for hours—DISGUSTING."

"I see. Yes, I understand. It's something we've been working on at home. I understand you have to keep to your policies. My job is all about policies." I felt a small, forced laugh catch in my throat before I heard it aloud. "Can we have just another week? I can't take time off, and it's just me." This last sentence earned Oliver's attention. Something had clicked in his mind in time with the cube he was slotting through the square hole. I uncrossed my arms and straightened my posture.

I used to be more careful. I'd model spelling out even borderline profane words like "ass" when friends came over to our apartment. But then I caught myself doing it at the bar when my friend Lisa asked me about my date with Brooks, and I said he was a *d-i-c-k*. I started talking to Oliver like an adult then, a correct decision given the listicle I later read titled, "5 Reasons You Should Say Goodbye to the Goo Goo Ga Ga's." This habit has prompted some looks from other parents at the park, but that's a small price to pay.

Before I left, I tried to think of a final zinger, but couldn't come up with anything better than, "I hope you're happy. Come on, Oliver. These people don't want us here."

⁂

The day after Oliver got kicked out of his preschool, he bit the little boy who lived in apartment six hard enough to leave a slobbery red mark. I was the host of our monthly Wedekind Apartment Wine and Dine, which served as an opportunity for us tenants to get together and complain about the creepy facilities guy, swap recipes, and drink too much without worrying about driving home.

This was the first time that I'd caught Oliver in the act, and the image was so unsettling that I instructed my memory bank to reject its deposit. The bite did not follow any kind of confrontation, which is why I didn't see it coming. As he wrapped his jaws around the boy's forearm and bit down, he kept his eyes wide open, only blinking after the nearest parent had pulled him from the other boy, who was screaming. The victim's mother picked him up and rushed to the bathroom. Over the muffled sound of screams and water rushing from the faucet, I told Oliver that he couldn't do that because it hurts, and he can't hurt other people. This was the first time I'd ever offered an explanation after the "Don't."

"Okay mommy," he said, and I didn't correct him to say "mom" like I normally did. That night, at the edge of sleep, I remembered the shark my biology class had been assigned to dissect in middle school. When Mr. Davis wasn't looking, some of the boys had plucked out and secreted away the shark's teeth to act as the crown jewels of their hemp necklaces.

Then, I thought about how Noah used to say my niece, Adriana, was so cute he could eat her up. I hated when he said it. I hated it when my own uncle said the same about five-year-old me. My uncle also used to squeeze above my knee, asking, "Who likes the boys?" until I finally conceded that it was me. I liked the boys. I didn't take Oliver around him for that reason.

The next morning, I tried to bake a loaf of pumpkin bread as an apologetic offering for the woman in number six. But as I got lost reading headlines about the Syrian civil war and a shooting at a nightclub, I realized that I hadn't set a timer. The bread was burnt, and a plume of smoke escaped from the oven when I opened it, triggering the alarm. Oliver started to yell in between the alarm's shrill beeps. He screamed for minutes after I'd disabled the alarm. Then, among the burnt pumpkin smell and the cries, I finally understood why a mother might hit her child. How could such a loud noise come from such a small body? As an infant, he'd hardly cried, but recently he'd begun to enter these states where he was completely inconsolable, where his inconsolability would crescendo to hysteria. He didn't throw tantrums over what other toddlers did—toys taken and dessert denied. Instead, he'd be set off by certain sounds or even temperatures. The tenant beneath me banged on the ceiling, and as he did, I felt my heartbeat pounding between my temples.

"Mom has a headache, sweetie. Please just shhh." I knelt down and squeezed Oliver's arms to his side as he continued to scream. Squeezing him only made him louder, an accordion with impossibly full bellows. Unable to absorb any more sound, I stood up quickly and lost my footing, which caused Oliver to topple over as well. He fell on his back and crumpled into a ball before falling silent, the only sound being my own panicked breathing. I explained that it was an accident, and I was sorry. I tried to unfurl his body to inspect for any markings of what I'd just done, but he didn't let me. He was a small comma punctuating the carpet. Maybe I could pack some candy in his lunch, I said. He loosened his grasp on his shins and sat up.

"Gummy bears," he declared, and observed my reaction. On the brink of my agreement, he clarified, "Sour gummy bears." I nodded though I didn't allow him to eat sour candies. They erode tooth enamel.

⁂

Oliver started at the new day care the next week, which had meant five days of me exhausting all possible caregiving options beforehand. On the day that I dropped him off with my uncle, I'd wished I could have called Noah instead, but dismissed the wish as one might dismiss a fleeting desire to upgrade a kitchen appliance in hopes of making life easier.

The new place was less expensive—no social emotional learning, but thankfully no Miss Emilys either—so I was able to pick up extra hours at work. I was promoted to lead moderator. It came with a fifty-cent-per-hour raise, which I spent several times over in my head before I actually received it.

Things were looking up. After that man died at his desk, they got better about giving us breaks throughout the day and decreasing our daily viewing load. When I was first hired, people told me I'd get used to the work, and I did. But not in the way they said I would. They said I would become numb, but I didn't. I still felt it all, but I felt it in double speed. I imagined my job as the VCR my parents had when I was growing up. I thought of the squeaky sound of tape between reels as actors' mouths flapped and limbs moved wildly when we rewound the videos. I hovered above my body and watched as time passed that body by, the only evidence of its forward march in the slowly deepening parentheses extending up from the corners of my mouth.

After Oliver's first day at the new day care, the lead toddler teacher Janine told me what a sweet boy he was. He was within earshot and appeared to hear her but carried on plinking on a toy xylophone. The sharp metallic sound continued to metronome in my mind hours after we left. I asked Oliver how his day was and if he learned anything new. He said, "Good," while shaking his head, and I wondered how these responses corresponded to the two questions.

For dinner, I made macaroni and cheese for Oliver and spaghetti for myself. At his baby shower, someone had gotten him a fork that, instead of having a straight handle, bent at a right angle—one of many gifts that weren't on my registry. This invention was designed to make it easier for kids to learn how to use utensils, but watching him use it unnerved me. He stabbed at his noodles with such force and imprecision that only a small fraction of his food actually made it to his mouth. I asked how he liked his dinner, and he frowned at the fallen elbow noodle that'd been precariously balanced on his fork before I interrupted his process.

I got him ready for bed, which was the best part of my day. We both respected the pre-bedtime rituals. If anything was done out of order, or there was any other disruption to the routine, neither of us slept well. One time, I'd gotten a sitter for a dinner date, which conflicted with the nighttime routine. I was so distracted by the dread of the routine's interruption that I couldn't focus on what the guy was saying. I kept checking my watch, which he interpreted to be the product of romantic disinterest rather than maternal concern (it was both). When I got home later that night, Oliver was already asleep. The babysitter gently reported that he was a handful as she smoothed the hairs that'd escaped the confines of her two French braids.

I hadn't baptized Oliver, but when I'd tilt his head back as he sat in the tub and shielded his eyes from the soapsuds, I sometimes liked to imagine that he was being purified and regenerated with each droplet of water, bringing him closer to being the fresh newborn who was so quiet that I thought he may not have survived his violent entrance into the world, which left me with a fourth degree tear that smarted with each of the wails that finally came.

As I got him ready for bed, I thought of one of the videos I had screened at work of a group of teenagers gathered in front of a Cinnabon, threatening to hurt a girl if she didn't give them her Snapchat handle. After a moment of chaotic silence, a boy with curly black hair threatened to split the girl in half. I flagged the video for removal—Excessively Violent Language—without watching the rest. I wondered if, when the boy was young, his mother had washed his hair with special shampoo to help maintain its curl.

Two weeks later, Noah reached out to me via the email address I reserved for junk mail and online shopping promo codes. My friends Lisa and Terry told me not to respond unless I was prepared to tell him about Oliver. But, after a night when three Long Island iced teas had washed away my inhibitions and better judgment, I sent him a short response where I asked how things were in Bristol and told him about my job screening videos. People had a fascination, reverence, and disgust for my work—the same way one might appreciate the meat delicately cut by a butcher's hand but be offended when he wore his bloodied apron in front of customers.

I wrote, "Want to move back to America yet?" and described a video taken during Black Friday where a man was trampled to death, his limp body left spooning the shiny white box of a 50-inch TV.

He responded moments after I sent the message, as I predicted he would. He was the kind of man who thought himself unknowable, but was easily understood, even by strangers. A nice man with something just slightly off, a man who might offer to bounce a fussy child on his knee as if his leg were a horse, the child its rider, but would keep his leg galloping even when the child was no longer having fun.

At a housewarming party once, he kept tugging on the dog's tail, which prompted a high-pitched bark from the dog and a few uncomfortable laughs from the attendants. After the third time, I held onto his hand and then squeezed it harder when I felt his hand moving in the direction of the dog.

"What?" he asked, his thick-lashed eyes just as wide open as the dog's. "It's funny."

"No, it's not," I mouthed in the same gentle, but forceful way I would to Oliver years later.

That is seriously fucked! he wrote, which steered our conversation in the direction I'd intended. He wanted more details about the videos, and I gleefully provided them until I realized that I was beginning to exaggerate things that didn't need exaggerating. We messaged back and forth throughout the night, and I started to miss the ease of our conversations, how he'd try so hard to make me laugh at the expense of his own self-respect. I sometimes imagined him with Oliver, repeating the same joke over and over without feeling embarrassed. Even when Oliver was a baby, I felt ashamed when I would make an effort to play a game of peekaboo and he would dismissively return to the more interesting view of the blank wall behind me.

But we could not be together because we did not love each other in a way that kept two people together. Or maybe I was worried that I loved him too much—needed him too much—that I saw in our relationship hints of my parents', where neither party could buy a pair of new pants without consulting the other first. I imagined myself asking him if he'd taken his pills and him making jokes about me being the only useful nag around.

Once, when I'd sprained my foot and had to use crutches, he took great care of me, fetching me glasses of water I didn't ask for and elevating my foot on a tower of pillows that was slightly too high. Eventually, though, his caretaking felt oppressive. At one point, the two full glasses of water rattled on the coffee table as he stomped around the apartment, grumbling about the importance of icing my foot and lamenting that we still used a damn ice tray.

He had moved to Bristol in order to be closer to his family, but I couldn't help but take the transcontinental move personally. Sometimes I wondered if his mother had a role in prompting the move. Whenever he got off of the phone with her, he looked impossibly weary; her words were always the heaviest ornament on the Christmas trees that weighed down the entire branch.

I revisited the question of telling Noah about Oliver, a question I had asked and answered hundreds of times already. The question was always the same, and the answer usually was too, unless I had a particularly difficult day with Oliver, in which case I liked to keep the possibility of a co-parent in the back of my mind like an emergency parachute. Considering the question once more, I answered like I normally did. No, I would not tell him. All parties involved were better off this way.

When I got to work the next day, the third email I opened described a new company policy, which would require us to watch each video at least twice to ensure that we weren't unfairly censoring material. Apparently, we'd come under fire for deleting sponsored content and needed to be more judicious in our decision-making, or we'd personally be responsible for the lost ad revenue. I knew that was an empty threat, but it still caused the same tension headache that a real threat would. But another email sent to me separately filled the empty threat. My supervisor explained that it was especially important that I take note of the new policy. In reviewing my logs, he had noticed a sizeable discrepancy between video lengths and the amount of time I spent watching them. If I made another error, I could be demoted, if not fired altogether.

Before loading my queue of videos for the day, I tucked in the bit of stomach flesh hanging over my khakis' waistband. I always bought my pants one size too small as punishment for not working hard enough to make parts of my post-baby body disappear. The tactic didn't really work, but seeing the pink lines laterally spanning the flesh beneath my belly button at least made me feel more proactive.

The first video was worse than a lot of the others I'd seen. A group of men wearing fatigues were throwing rocks at a group of women kneeling on prayer rugs. Their guns swung across their backs as they threw, taking steps backward from their targets in a game I didn't understand. I nearly clicked on the button to ban it—Excessive or Targeted Violence—but remembered that we needed to watch the video more than once before making a decision. On the second viewing, I saw that one of the women had already been hit, and bright red dripped from the tip of her nose. I wasn't able to do my usual trick of mentally speeding up the videos to transform my day into a blur of images. This one moved in slow motion so that I felt like I could hear the droplets of blood as they fell. This time, I couldn't stop watching.

A man laughed as a rock bounced off someone's bowed head, and he loudly instructed a young boy to bring him more rocks, modeling the shape and size of rocks he wanted. The boy diligently began collecting stones in a way that reminded me of Oliver, who flourished when he was following rules—or when he was pointing out that others were not following rules.

I flagged the video and made a note of the blood and the prayer mats in the newly added "reason for decision" box that accompanied it, before claiming my wellness time early. My hand shook as I poured myself a cup of coffee that I didn't want. As I stood in the closet that'd been retrofitted with a table, two chairs, and a microwave to become a break room, I tried to remember the last time I'd seen Oliver laugh. I couldn't recall a single instance. My mind was playing tricks on me, I think. In that office, under those fluorescent lights, my mind did not allow me to access any joyful memories. Those were checked at the front door near the employee parking lot, and they came flooding back to me whenever I left for the day. Even when it was cloudy outside, it felt as if the sky cracked open to let the sun's rays come through, and I breathed in the relief that the horrors I'd seen lived in some terrible, faraway place I got paid to visit.

⁂

The following Wednesday, I took Oliver to an animated movie about a troll named Jötunn who didn't know his own strength. This was supposed to be a stand-in for a lesson I didn't know how to teach, and as Oliver watched the bright screen, I watched the light bounce off his face. While the other kids in the theater spoke at full volume, asking questions about the characters and repeating lines, Oliver sat silently. I replenished his bucket of popcorn, a miniature replica of my own, as his fingers neared the bottom. He had stopped biting other kids, but Janine described a couple of instances where he pulled on ponytails and pinched bare legs. Nothing I should worry about, she assured me. All normal behaviors for boys his age.

At the end of the movie, Jötunn met another troll his same size, and they were able to roughhouse without either one getting hurt. As we left the theater, I asked if Oliver liked the movie, and he said he did. I thanked him for sitting still throughout the whole movie and said this could be our new tradition. Oliver nodded and traced patterns in the theater's stucco façade as we walked.

I heard a child crying in the parking lot and found the source in a minivan parked right next to our car. A man was threatening to spank his child again if he didn't stop crying. I squeezed Oliver's hand tighter, as if holding onto him could strengthen my own resolve to intervene. I thought about the fact that, if recorded, this scene would never be flagged for removal.

"Excuse me, sir," I said, gesturing to my car's door. The man had wide shoulders, and his muscles flexed beneath a T-shirt thinned from too many washes.

"What?" he barked, moving his arms in and out of the sliding door in a way that made it seem like he was shaking something, or someone. The crying had stopped, and I hoped he was resolving some mechanical issue with a seatbelt buckle or fishing for a dropped pacifier. I also hoped the awareness of my observing him would be enough to make the man reconsider the way he treated his child. I tried to see inside the van, but the window's dark tint and the man's body positioning made the entire situation opaque.

"Please," I said. "There's not enough room." He slid the door shut and pressed his body into his van to permit access to Oliver's car seat. He said something in the tone of an apology, but I couldn't quite hear. In later versions of this memory, revised by a sour guilt, he apologized to his child instead of me.

"Did that make you scared?" I asked Oliver once we were safely locked into our own car.

"Yes," he said, and I saw that he'd begun to cry. I sped away and turned on a song we both knew the words to.

During our bedtime routine that night, I ran his bathwater a little hotter than usual and added too much bubble bath solution. Bubbles formed in mounds above the water. When the bath had cooled enough for Oliver to enter, I let him hide away behind the highest mound, constructing his own sudsy fortress.

ACKNOWLEDGMENTS

These stories have been many years in the writing, and I am beyond grateful to my fellow writers, mentors, friends, and family members who supported me as I worked to get them out into the world.

Thank you to my writing group members who provided insightful feedback on nearly all of the work in this collection: Satoshi Tabuchi, Anna Reeser, and Emily Mathis. I'm so glad our writing/life paths crossed during that overcast weekend in Newport, Oregon. Thanks also to Lauren Hughes for some key editorial feedback and encouragement as I completed final revisions.

Thanks to the journals who first served as homes for some of the stories in this collection:

"Fire Season": *phoebe*

"Backscatter": *december*

"Alternate Route Suggested": *Bull*

"Artifacts Worth Saving": *Green Mountains Review*

Thank you to Curtis Vickers, who first championed this manuscript, as well as the current University of Nevada Press team: Ryan Masteller, JoAnne Banducci, and Caddie Dufurrena.

Will Burrows, thank you for designing a cover that captured this book's essence.

Thank you to fellow writer Kate McIntyre for such a generous reading of my book. Your incredible ability to make places feel like characters in your collection inspired many of the details in these stories.

To the people associated with UNR's MFA program, thank you for giving me grace as I worked to find my writing voice: Raluca Balasa, Matt Baker, Linzy Garcia, Rachel Chimits, Molly Beckwith, Laura Valenza, Danielle Mayabb, Michelle Wait, Casey Bell, Brian Rowe, Joanne Mallari, Nate Perry, and Chris Coake.

Thank you, Mizzou Crew, for encouraging me and keeping me accountable throughout the PhD program: my mentors, Phong Nguyen and Trudy Lewis, and my fellow writers, Bailey Gaylin Moore, Sam Edmonds, and Hayli Cox.

Thanks to my friends: Lauren Bateman for being my fiercest advocate and fellow lol-er, Phoebe Judge for sticking by my side from awkward adolescence to slightly-less-awkward adulthood, and Caylin Capra-Thomas for inspiring me through your brilliant wit and teaching me that "jokes are ideas."

Thank you to the people who've experienced Reno in all of its strange beauty—dive bars and alleyways, sun-dried foothills and cloudless skies—with me over the years: Morgan Greenwood, Rebecca Reighard, Timber Weiss, Laura Reaney, Kelly Burrows, and Tia Corder.

Thank you to my husband, Orlin, who both grounds me and raises me up, making it easier to continue moving forward, even after I stumble.

Thanks to my siblings, my first and forever friends: Mark, Chris, Amanda, Zac, Alison, Jonathan, and Matthew. Thanks, Dad, for teaching me by doing. I so admire you for your love of adventure and insatiable appetite for new experiences.

This book is dedicated to my mom, who saved every story I ever wrote and inspired me to find humor in the absurd and joy in the act of observing. If you were still with us, I like to think that you'd save these ones too.

ABOUT THE AUTHOR

AnnElise Hatjakes holds a PhD in creative writing from the University of Missouri and an MFA in fiction from the University of Nevada, Reno, where she currently teaches English. Her stories have been short-listed for the Neil Shepard Prize in Fiction and the Curt Johnson Prize and have appeared in journals including *Juked*, *phoebe*, *Bull*, *Tahoma Literary Review*, and *Typehouse*, among others.